W•CLARK
PUBLISHING

GUN SMOKE

A Novel by

KAYLIN SANTOS

Wahida Clark Presents Publishing
60 Evergreen Place
Suite 904
East Orange, New Jersey 07018
973-678-9982
www.wclarkpublishing.com

Gunsmoke by Kaylin Santos
ISBN 13-digit 978-1936649365
ISBN 10-digit 1936649365

Library of Congress Cataloging-In-Publication Data:
LCCN 2013902553
    1. Street Lit   2. African American Fiction
    3. Urban Fiction 4. Philadelphia, PA 5. Illegal Dog
    Fighting   6. Gambling 7. Prostitution   8. Atlantic City,
    NJ

Cover design and layout by Nuance Art.*.
Book design by NuanceArt@wclarkpublishing.com
Proofreader Rosalind Hamilton
Sr. Editor Linda Wilson

ACKNOWLEDGEMENTS

All Praise is Forever Due to the Beneficent, the Most Merciful. Angel, my soul mate thank you for being you. Jahara our daughter is growing up to be just like you. To My son Malik, I am so proud of you.

Angel, thank you for this book challenge. You didn't think I could do it, did you? ☺ Let's see who sells the most copies.

Wahida Clark, thank you for breathing life into us and building our platform.

DEDICATION

*To my brother, Kyron Devon Santos. R.I.P.
We both did what we had to do.*

GUN SMOKE

A NOVEL BY
KAYLIN SANTOS

Chapter 1

Dog fights and gambling went hand and hand at Lauryn's spot. She sat at the mini bar entertaining one of her high rollers who had been upstairs gambling for six hours straight before coming up for air. It was typical for Lauryn, to also be the host some nights at her small time casino. She really didn't mind hosting, nor did she mind all the attention her 38 DD breasts got either, just as long as those puppies kept niggas wanting to gamble at her place.

"We got a problem," Simair whispered to Lauryn as she poured the high roller another drink.

Lauryn quickly got up and followed Simair toward the basement where the lights were dim, and the sound of barking dogs filled the air. When she made her way down the steps, she noticed only one dog in the dog ring, and a small crowd stood behind Mark, the owner of the dog. Normally, there would be two dogfights per day in her establishment, but today there wasn't one person trying to put their dog up against Mark's dog, Busta. "What's goin' on down here?" she asked nonchalantly as she stepped into the ring.

"Don't nobody wanna fight," Mark shot back in an aggressive tone. He looked over at the two would-be dogfighters who backed out after seeing what they were up against. "I got 10K that my dog will kill anything that steps in this ring."

Lauryn looked shocked and even chuckled at the amount of money that Mark was willing to bet on his dog. The average dogfighter wouldn't bet any less than 15K per fight, of which 10% of the winnings would go to the house. She scanned the room and calculated the potential side bets before determining that she would entertain this wager, along with any other bets that rode with Busta.

She stepped out of the ring and walked toward the back where she slid open a door that was cut off from the rest of the basement. Lying there on a mattress was Lady, a red nose pit bull who was in the middle of nursing her puppies. Lauryn didn't have to say a word as Lady rose to her feet, wagging her tail, happy to see her owner. Side by side, they both walked to the ring with one thing on their mind . . . kill!

"Fuck am I supposed to do with this?" Mark asked, looking at the playful, frail female dog as she jumped into the ring.

"What? You said nobody wants to fight. I'll see ya 10K and I'll take all side bets!" Lauryn yelled out to the spectators. "Fight to the death! Round one. No clock. Being as though you got a male dog, there's no odds. Straight bets," Lauryn announced.

Mark thought Lauryn was crazy, but he acted fast in pulling out the 10K and passed it over to her. He knew there had to be something special about Lady, but he decided to go with his gut instinct. *There is no way in hell that Busta's gonna lose this fight,* he thought.

Lauryn pulled her long black hair into a ponytail, kneeled down and gave Lady a kiss on the top of her head. Simair began collecting money from the side bettors, and within a minute, the ring was clear and the fight was ready to begin.

Busta stood there barking and pulling at the chain that held him back. Lady just sat there looking confused and scared, with her tail tucked between her legs as though she wanted nothing else but to get out of the ring. Standing in front of her petite-sized owner, didn't make Lady look too convincing either.

A motion from Lauryn to Mark signaling him to let his dog off the leash was all it took. Within the blink of an eye, Busta was all over Lady, and had locked onto the back of her neck with jaw-crushing force.

Lauryn looked on without saying a word. While Mark, on the other hand, continued to yell out, "Kill! Kill!"

"*Defensa!*" Lauryn spoke to Lady in Spanish, calmly telling her to defend her neck.

Lady quickly gave Busta her back, and the tail that was tucked between her legs sprang out and began to wag. Busta continued shaking the back of Lady's neck, refusing to unlock his grip.

Mark looked over at Lauryn with victory in his eyes, but was confused by the giggles that she and Simair shared while looking down at the two dogs.

Lady was only toying around with Busta, and her wagging tail showed her playfulness. But playtime was over. Lauryn knew that Lady was a little weak from nursing her puppies and had to end the fight quickly.

"*Castigado!*" Lauryn said. *Pierna! Pierna!*" she instructed Lady to punish Busta.

Lady immediately got low to the ground and went for Busta's two front legs. Busta tried to tuck in both of his legs, but only saved one. Lady bit down on the other one, forcing him to loosen his grip on her neck, which was all she needed.

"*Huevos!*" Lauryn finally yelled out, seeing an opening.

In one swift jolt, Lady released Busta's leg, darted up under his body, and locked onto his balls. The agonizing pain shot through Busta's body so sharply that he never thought twice about trying to bite back. He howled at the top of his lungs, and his cries echoed throughout the basement.

Hearing the word, *"Matalo!"* spoken by her master, Lady knew that meant "kill". She yanked and yanked at Busta's balls until the skin started to break.

The bystanders grabbed a hold of their own nuts and turned away, knowing what was about to happen next.

Lady yanked until she ripped his balls off, and when she did, she dropped them on the floor and went right back for Busta's dick.

That was enough. Mark couldn't take anymore. He pulled a .38 snub nose from his back pocket, aimed it at Busta and pulled the trigger. But he didn't stop there. He kept squeezing the trigger, striking Lady in her head in the process. By the time he emptied the revolver, Lauryn and Simair were aiming a pair of twin Glock .40's at his head. Not only was Mark out of pocket, but he was also out of bullets.

It was one thing to fire off shots in the casino, but it was a whole other ballpark killing the only true friend that Lauryn had outside of her family. Her mind was racing, and all she wanted to do was blow Mark's head off. For a second she pictured his brains splattered all over the spectators behind him. Her desire to kill him was suppressed by the the kind of heat a dead body in the basement of an illegal casino would bring; not to mention the many witnesses looking on.

Lauryn lowered her gun, but Simair was reluctant to do the same. He was unwilling to let Mark leave the basement. "Clean dis shit up and get dis dickhead out of here!" Lauryn said as she lowered Simair's gun. "Basement's closed!" she announced to the spectators.

Lauryn looked down at Lady one last time before turning around and walking up the basement steps, holding back the tears filling her eyes.

GUN SMOKE

Mark stood there with a stupid look on his face, regretting what he had just done. He knew beyond a shadow of doubt that this wasn't going to be the end of this situation.

Chapter 2

T he small warehouse just off I-95 was the designated place for the transactions of illegal goods. Waiting inside the warehouse were two U-Haul trucks, six armed men, and one Jewish investor named Base.

Base was from New Jersey, and he owned a factory that made tabletop games for Atlantic City casinos. He did brisk legit business, but his more lucrative transactions were his dealings with the mob and small illegal casino owners like Lauryn. But Base knew if the Gaming Committee found out, they would have Base's Jewish ass for dinner, and destroy his career, along with whoever else was involved. He and his men had been awaiting the arrival of Sayyon, who had just pulled up into the loading dock.

Sayyon and Boonchie pulled up in all white Cadillac truck. Sayyon was Lauryn's youngest brother and also the most rambunctious. Lauryn had spoiled him with the good life, but now that he was older, he was anxious to get out of his sister's shadow.

Sayyon jumped out of the truck, adjusting the seventeen shot Beretta on his waist. At 6 feet tall and 230 pounds solid, one could understand why Base was so cautious around him. Every time Sayyon did business with Base, there was always tension in the air. It mostly came from Base, who sometimes felt threatened by blacks, especially blacks with guns just as big as his.

Base watched the two men exit the white Cadillac truck. Although Boonchie was short and stubby, the fully automatic AR-15 he was toting wasn't. He was a well-known body snatcher, known to let it rip, and he didn't have time to be playing games. Boonchie looked like he had just come from SWAT training, and Base couldn't help but respect the young man who stood behind the large gun. He looked back at his own men, as if to say, "Step ya game up!" being as though they were only packing semi-automatic handguns.

"Is all that necessary?" Base quipped, tone dripping with sarcasm.

Sayyon used his finger to do an exaggerated head count of all Base's men.

"Is all that?" Sayyon snorted, glancing back at his men.

"I was expecting maybe Simair or your sister, you know, somebody with some authority?"

A couple of Base's men snickered. Sayyon's temperature simmered.

"I'm saying, Hitler, you wanna play games or do business?" Sayyon shot back.

"Fuck you!" Base roared, because Sayyon hit a nerve. "Fuck you!"

Base's men visibly stiffened. Boonchie lifted his AR-15 and cradled it to his chest. The tension mounted. Base saw the young boys weren't to be intimidated, so he motioned to his men to stand down.

"Ay, no harm done, eh? You want business, let's do business." Base smiled.

Base escorted them to the back of the two trucks. Boonchie kept his distance along with a watchful eye already calculating the first, second, and third person he was going to shoot in the event that any one of them did something stupid.

Base slid open the door to the first truck, and then the next one, revealing its contents.

"Over here I got the craps table you ordered," he said, pointing to the first truck. "I also have a blackjack table and a Russian roulette table if you're interested."

Sayyon was only there to buy the craps table. He knew if he came back with anything more, Lauryn would definitely give him the business. She had a way with words, and even though Sayyon was her baby brother, she pulled no punches when it came down to her business.

"Naw, just give me the craps table," Sayyon replied.

"I can give you a good deal," Base baited as he lit up a smoke.

Sayyon stopped.

"How good?"

Base's smiled and thought, *Got 'im.*

"Give me 12K for everything."

All tabletop games were five grand apiece, so 12K was definitely a good deal. Sayyon scratched his head, and then looked at Boonchie for advice, but Boonchie's eyes were locked on the other men.

"What's the matter, kid? Need to talk to sis first?" Base asked with a straight face.

Sayyon knew he was testing his gangsta, but deep down, he was tired of asking sis. He was a man, his own man.

Fuck it, Sayyon thought, thinking of the financial gain.

"You got yourself a deal," he replied.

He pulled out the money and counted off twelve grand.

"Tell your drivers to follow me," he added.

If Lauryn got mad, so what, because Sayyon was ready to step out on his own and set up his own operation. More than likely he was gonna put the extra craps table, the Russian roulette table, and the extra slot machine into storage until he figured out what to do with them.

Base sensed the independent streak in Sayyon and wanted to use it to his advantage. He took Sayyon aside once the deal was done. "Look, kid, I hope you don't take it personal, me bustin' your balls earlier. Just my way of feeling you out."

"I never take business personal," Sayyon replied.

"That's good because I've got a business offer for you and just you. Something you and I can connect on."

"Like what?"

"Not right now. I'll give you a call, eh? Trust me, it'll be worth your while," Base assured him.

They shook hands and Base smiled to himself because he could see the greed in Sayyon's eyes.

Chapter 3

T he sound of heavy barking cut through the air as Mark sat in his backyard feeding his dogs. He was originally from North Philly, but he rested his head in Mount Airy, the uptown section of the city. He had a pretty nice house with a large enough backyard to house a variety of pit bulls.

Mark was so distracted by the barking dogs that he didn't notice or hear the two people making their way up the driveway and straight toward the rear of the house. The sound of the Dog Chow hitting the empty bowls came to a halt when the presence of two individuals standing behind him caught his attention. "Who da fuck gave you permission to come onto my property?" he asked, tossing the bag of dog food to the ground and taking the latch off one of the dog cages.

Then, an all too familiar voice spoke out, causing the hair on Mark's arms to stand up. "I did!" As he looked over his shoulder to confirm the owner of the voice, Lauryn stood there, wearing a pair of Gucci shades, a white tank top, blue jeans and a pair of open-toe Steve Madden heels. Simair stood right next to her, clutching a chrome .38 snub nose that quickly got his attention.

Lauryn smiled and knelt down. She was amused by Mark's antics at releasing one of his dogs when he took the latch off the cage. "Come here!" she said softly, which caused the dog to charge out of the cage. Mark knew for sure that Pebbles, an all-white American pit bull, was about to

chew Lauryn a new asshole. Simair even pointed his gun
directly at the dog with the intention of shooting it before it
got the chance to bite her.

Lauryn waved Simair off and stuck her hand out to the
dog just as it reached her. Its two front paws dug into the
ground as it stopped and kicked up a little dirt on her clothes.
No longer in attack mode, Pebbles' tail wagged
uncontrollably with every stroke that Lauryn gave to the side
of her body.

Embarrassed, Mark put his head down in disappointment
at his prized fighting dog.

"See, Mark. Us bitches stick together!" Lauryn said,
sitting Pebbles down in front of her.

Mark had no idea how much Lauryn loved dogs, and
more specifically, her best friend, Lady, whom Mark had no
problem killing right before her eyes. Lauryn took that
personally for several reasons, which brought her to where
she was right now. Mark had no respect for her, her club, the
bystanders, and most importantly, her dog.

"Like I said, what da fuck you want?" Mark shot back at
her, but this time in a more aggressive manner.

Simair passed Lauryn the .38 he had in his hand.

"Oh, you gonna shoot me?" Mark asked, thinking she was
bluffing. "Bitch, you ain't got it in you," he said, taking a few
steps toward her.

Mark underestimated Lauryn's pretty face, thinking she
was sweet with her beauty. He took a step toward her and
Pebbles started to growl.

Pebbles' reaction made Mark furious. He was so furious
that he leaned over and grabbed a rock the size of a
grapefruit and started to throw it at the dog. But as he raised
his arm, the first shot hit him in the abdomen, causing the
rock to fall out of his hand. He grabbed his stomach and

looked at Lauryn in shock. "Bitch, you shot me!" he said, taking his hand from his stomach to look at the blood on his hand.

This wasn't a game. Lauryn was serious. As crazy as it seemed, she valued the life of her dog more than Mark's life, but at the same time, she wasn't going to kill him like he killed Lady. A shit-bag shot was good enough to leave a permanent scar, as was left on Lauryn's heart when he shot Lady. Mark wasn't much of a threat, and only a few people in North Philly messed with him. So if Mark did decide to retaliate, he would more than likely be alone, and in Lauryn's eyes, one person was always easier to kill than a few. For now, he was going to be an example, and examples were always needed to keep the rules and regulations of the club in order.

Mark stood there waiting to see if Lauryn was done, because if she was, he had already made up his mind that they wouldn't make it off his property. A gun lay on his kitchen counter a mere two-feet from the back door that led out to the yard. Whatever was going to happen needed to happen now, because he was feeling a little woozy from the amount of blood he was losing.

Lauryn stood up, walked over and grabbed one of the leashes and a harness off the top of a dog cage. The .38 remained in her hand the entire time, so when she walked past Mark, he didn't think twice about doing anything to her. He was concerned about what she was going to do with the leash, but even more concerned with the way his stomach started to feel.

"Yo, just get out of here!" Mark said.

"I told you, us bitches gotta stick wit' each other," Lauryn uttered, placing the harness on Pebbles. "Don't let me catch you in my club again. Next time it'll be a head shot instead of your stomach." She turned and walked out of the backyard with Pebbles in tow.

Mark waited until they crossed the threshold of the backyard before he made his way to the kitchen. He wanted to run toward the back door, but nullified his action due to the burning in his stomach, so he was only able to walk slowly. As he finally reached the kitchen, he could see Lauryn at the front of the house. Suddenly, he started seeing double. Something was seriously wrong. Instead of reaching for his gun, he reached for the cell phone beside it and dialed 911 as fast as his slow fingers could dial. He couldn't even stand anymore and dropped to his knees.

"Nine-one-one!" the operator said into the phone.

"I've been shot! Da bitch shot me!" he uttered into the phone before passing out.

* * * * * *

"It's not here! I don't see anything!" Trinity yelled from the back of the cargo van. "It's just a bunch of bullshit back here!" she told Missy, who sat in the passenger seat smoking a cigarette.

"Just keep looking. I know it's there," Missy instructed Trinity while she kept her eyes and her gun on the driver.

Born and partly raised in West Philly, Missy migrated to Brooklyn at the age of sixteen due to her father kicking her out of the house after finding out that she was pregnant on her fifteenth birthday. She stayed in Philly until she had the baby, and then fled for the big city, but not before leaving her baby on her father's front doorstep. The moment she walked away from her baby, her heart became hardened. Twenty-four years later, she had been in everything but a hearse while terrorizing the city of New York with a harsh combination of beauty, brains, and an orgasmic addiction to squeezing the trigger.

The man sitting in the driver's seat of the van was zip-tied to the steering wheel, bleeding from the gash at the side of his face from Missy repeatedly pistol-whipping him. He wondered how he let himself be suckered into giving these trifling bitches a ride, but one look at them told the story.

Missy stood 5-feet 9-inches and 150 pounds. She had an amazing body equipped with 36D breasts, a 24-inch waist and 36-inch ass. Her light brown skin was complemented by her pretty brown eyes, a sprinkling of freckles and irresistible dimples. She didn't look a day over twenty-five even though she was pushing forty.

Far from a slouch herself, Trinity was a 5-foot-7 Dominican devil with a petitie frame, full pouty lips, and Eva Mendes type beauty.

They had approached the driver as he got gas.

"Going our way, Big Daddy?" Missy sang with a 'come fuck me' look on her face.

The driver was stuck from jump.

"If I wasn't, I am now," he gulped, eyeing the two beauties like he had just hit the jackpot.

Or more like crapped out.

As soon as they pulled off from the bright lights of the gas station, Missy put the gun to his head.

"Fuck up, and this will be the only blow job you get," Missy hissed.

"What the fuck? I ain't got nothing!"

He had no idea that she was already ten steps ahead of him, and knew the exact contents he was delivering across town. She directed him to a back street, and then proceeded to beat him bloody.

"Please don't hit me no more! I don't have anything!" he begged.

"Okay." Missy shrugged, cocking back the hammer. "Then you about to die for nothin."

Hearing the word die brought him to his senses.

"It's in the walls! The money is in the walls!" he blurted out, spitting blood on the windshield in the process.

Missy smiled and pinched his bloody cheek.

"See? Now was that so hard?" she asked, before bashing him once more over the head and knocking him into a state of semi-consciousness.

Missy climbed out of the seat and into the back of the van, and then began pulling the paneling off the walls, with Trinity's help.

The word, "Jackpot!" silenced the noise of the walls being ripped away. Trinity was first to spot one of the many two-foot bundles of money. Missy then found the same on the other side of the van. Bundle after bundle, they pulled money out of the walls. There was a lot more than Missy thought was going to be there. In fact, this might be the biggest sting she'd done in her life. Jackpot was an understatement. This was the mother lode!

"All right, Roscoe," Missy said as she climbed back into the front seat. "Now that we got that out of the way, here's the deal pertaining to whether or not you're gonna live through this. I'm not a bad person, so we'll play Rock, Paper, Scissors. Best three out of five. You win, you live. You lose . . . well, you know what happens if you lose," she said, lifting his head off the steering wheel with her gun.

First, Roscoe didn't feel like playing any kid's game with her, especially with his life. Before he could express his disgust with the idea, she was already pumping her fist, and played scissors for the first round. Although Roscoe was zip-tied to the steering wheel, he still could move his hands, but he decided not to play anyway.

"One to nothing!" Missy announced, taking the safety off her gun. "One, two, three!" She began again and pumped her fist and played paper for the second round.

This was getting out of hand. Roscoe wasn't the least bit amused at the childish game and losing yet another round. "You crazy bitch! Let me the fuck go!" he shouted when he saw that Missy was serious. He watched her pump her fist for the third round, and the count to three was so fast that he almost lost the final round. Missy played rock this time, and in the nick of time he played paper, not wanting to look down the barrel of the gun that was going to blow his head off if he didn't play.

"Two to one!" Missy said with a smile on her face. She was intrigued that he decided to play the game. "One, two, three!" she yelled out and played scissors for round four.

Roscoe played paper, but quickly changed it to rock once he realized that she was playing scissors. He was fast, but not fast enough to get over on her. "I played rock! I played rock!" he yelled, hoping she didn't catch him.

While Missy was playing her game with Roscoe, Trinity was outside loading the money into her black Buick Regal. She was used to Missy's crazy antics, being as though she hung around her every day for the past two years. Missy was like her mentor, and at the ripe young age of twenty, the forty-year-old Missy was teaching her everything she knew about the streets, and how to get money on a higher level. Nothing was beyond belief when it came to Missy, so when Trinity heard the shot erupt from the van, it came as no surprise to her that Missy had just killed Roscoe.

"Damn, bitch! You ain't done yet?" Missy joked as she stepped out of the van and adjusted her miniskirt and fixed her hair.

Chapter 4

G ood afternoon, gentlemen," Assistant District Attorney Pamela Graham announced as she walked into the conference room where Special Agent Tony Razor and Assistant United States Attorney Jeffery Wilkes sat.

Anytime things got too far out of hand and the State couldn't control the situation, they would call in someone who was well equipped and well funded to pick up the slack. Lauryn Brown was getting to be a little too much for them. She was running her small North Philly club as a profitable casino. The State knew beyond a shadow of a doubt that illegal activities were taking place inside the establishment. But every time they sent an informant in to help gather evidence, they either ended up being turned away at the door, or for the one who did make it in, he never came back out . . . at least not out of the front door anyway.

"Her name is Lauryn Marie Brown, a North Philly native," Pamela said while passing small folders across the table to the well-suited men. "About four years ago we locked up one of North Philadelphia's biggest drug distributors named Jamal Nixon, aka Baby Neno. He left an undisclosed amount of money, drugs, and weapons that we were unable to locate during the search and seizures. His girlfriend was one, Lauryn Brown," Pamela said, pointing to Lauryn's photo.

"Well, how do you know he left everything with her?" the agent asked, cutting in as he looked through the contents in the file.

"A reliable informant from inside the small organization told us about it, but through many attempts, we've tried to catch her in the act of committing a crime, but she'd always be one step ahead of us." Pam went on, getting a little frustrated just thinking about it. "She bought a row house on the 2500 block of Bouvier Street in North Philly, which she legally turned into an afterhours spot. Rumor has it that she turned it into a mini casino. Besides illegal gambling, we have been advised that other criminal activities are going on inside. We just have a few legal obstacles preventing us from breaking down the door and locking everybody up. No judge in the State courts would issue a warrant without probable cause."

The Feds sat and listened to Pamela break down a RICO case in the federal system. Cases like this one, that might seem small and unimportant to the State, allowed the Feds to have a field day, especially when they took down twenty-man organizations. They were getting irritated just listening to Pamela, and wondered why they weren't called earlier. Legal obstacles that prevented the State from building a case wouldn't be an obstacle at all for the Feds. They are the best at what they do. After Pamela broke down the entire situation, Agent Brandon Razor was thirsty for the convictions, and so was Wilkes.

"Oh, and before you guys leave, I have something else to tell you," Pam said as she tucked her paperwork into her briefcase. "Neno made parole 45 days ago. He should be in a halfway house any day now. Keep in mind, we're talking about one of the bigger drug dealers Philly has ever seen. His return to the streets will be our biggest problem!"

GUN SMOKE

Lauryn pulled up into the bus terminal in Manhattan, pretty much tired from the two and a half hour drive from Philly. Her grandfather had gone off on yet another one of his journeys and was unable to find his way home. He had Stage-3 Alzheimer's disease, and if not closely watched, he was liable to travel to the other side of the map, which he almost did on a couple of occasions.

Mr. George was Lauryn's maternal grandfather. Lauryn never knew her mother, and only got a glimpse of her when she was around ten years of age. From the couple of stories that she heard about her mother, she could only remember the one about her death, which her father told her of before he passed away himself. All Lauryn had in her life from the age of thirteen was her grandfather, and he took care of her the best way he could.

"Pop-Pop, not again!" Lauryn said as she walked into the small room that the bus station security placed him in. "You can't keep going off like this," she said in a concerned manner, helping him to his feet.

"What's your name, little girl?" he replied as if he had no idea who Lauryn was.

Just seeing her grandfather in this condition made her cry. She was always afraid that one day he might go off and never come back home, or even worse, end up dead somewhere in a ditch. That somewhere would most likely be in New York, because that's where she would always pick him up when he wandered off. She would have to drive to Brooklyn, the Bronx, Queens, or Manhattan. She just thanked God for Mr. George's tracking device.

During the drive back home, Mr. George kept talking about going to visit his daughter in New York whose name he kept saying was "Modest". It didn't make any sense because he had only one biological daughter, Lauryn's mother, and her name was Nahja Dover. Nothing that came out of her grandfather's mouth made any sense, but at this point it really didn't matter. Lauryn loved him beyond his disability and would travel all the way to China to pick him up.

* * * * * *

"Mr. Tucker, do you know who shot you? Do you know who shot you, sir?" one of the detectives asked repeatedly.

Mark had been through multiple surgeries all night long. The bullet had ripped through his stomach and knocked off a large chunk of his liver. The wound was a fatal one, and as badly as the doctors tried to put him back together, no one in the room was optimistic about his recovery.

"Stay with me, Mr. Tucker . . . stay with me!" the doctor yelled as Mark slowly began fading away.

He couldn't do it. The wound was too severe and his body couldn't take it anymore.

The sound of the heart monitor flat lining was the breaking point for the doctor, who was unable to stop the excessive bleeding. He quickly yelled for the paddles in a last attempt to save Mark. "Clear!" he yelled before sending several hundred volts of electricity through Mark's body. "Clear!" he yelled out again, shocking Mark's heart in hopes of getting a heartbeat and pulse.

The doctor looked over at the detective and shook his head. It was over. Mark had died without ever naming the person who had shot him. All he had said in between surgeries was, "Dat bitch shot me!" It wasn't enough for the detectives in the room, but it was a start.

"Time of death, 5:36 a.m.," the doctor announced, looking up at the clock on the wall. Then came the hardest part of any doctor's job, and that was going out into the waiting room and telling the family that he was unable to save their loved one.

Chapter 5

S ayyon slid Bianca's panties down as he laid her across his bed. He gazed down at her soft chocolate skin.

"You know you my heart, right?" Sayyon crooned.

Bianca squirmed under his gaze.

"I love you, Sayyon."

Bianca had been his girl for three years, ever since her sixteenth birthday. Sayyon bagged her because she reminded him of Kelly Roland of Destiny's child and they had been together ever since. He kissed down the length of her bra, pausing at her fat juicy nipples, licking from one to the other and making her moan and grab his head. When he reached her belly button, Bianca applied subtle pressure urging him lower until his tongue tasted the tip of her clit.

"Ohhh, Say—" was all she got out before he slid his tongue inside her pussy lips and began tongue fucking her relentlessly.

She cocked her legs wider and she arched her back, rotating her hips. He licked and sucked on that pussy until she came all over his mouth, giving him a milk moustache.

"Fuck, baby, this pussy on fire," she groaned, licking her lips lustfully.

Sayyon gripped the base of his eight-inch banana curved dick and pushed it deep inside of Bianca, taking her breath away and making her wrap her legs around his waist. He pinned her legs behind his arms, long dicking Bianca fast and furious in a pushup position.

"Yes, baby, that's my—my spot!" she squealed.

"Throw it back, baby. Take this dick," he gritted.

"I-I am!" Bianca replied, meeting him thrust for thrust.

Sayyon was at an angle where he was hitting pure pussy, and Bianca was taking every inch like a pro. He felt the rumble in his stomach and it made him bang her harder.

"Sayyon, cum in your pussy! Cum deep in this pussy, baby!"

He felt the explosion in his toes, filling her with his seed.

"Damn, you feel so good," Sayyon said, kissing and sucking on Bianca's lips.

"I'm supposed to. You're home, right?"

"No doubt, lil mama. I love you."

"I love you, too."

Sayyon's phone interrupted their tender moment.

"Don't answer it," she whined.

"I have to, ma," he replied, grunting as he reached over and grabbed his pants off the floor.

Once he grabbed the phone, he rolled off Bianca and answered.

"Yo."

"Sayyon?"

"Yeah, who this?" he growled.

"Who do you think it is?"

Sayyon finally caught the voice. It was Base.

"Yeah, I know who it is. What's good?"

"Remember that deal I wanted to talk about?" Base reminded him.

"Yeah."

"It's goin' down. What do you think about that white girl?"

"That white girl?" Sayyon repeated with a frown; then it hit him.

"Ohh, you mean—"

Base cut him off.

"Yeah. Yeah, kid. That. Remember we on the phone. Can you be at Outback's in twenty minutes?"

"No doubt."

"Good to hear. I'll be waiting."

Sayyon hung up.

"Nigga, I know you don't think you 'bout to leave me and go see some white girl," Bianca sassed.

Sayyon laughed as he put on his pants.

"Naw, ma. It ain't about no white girl."

"Then why he say—" she started to say, and then it hit her. "Uh-uh, Sayyon. You talkin' about . . . cocaine?"

Sayyon stood up, throwing on his shirt.

"Just chill yo, it ain't that serious."

"Ain't that serious? Sayyon, I thought we were going to college and get away from this bullshit!"

"We are, baby," he assured her, sitting down and caressing her leg.

"So why are you jeopardizing your life, our life, when you don't have to? You're not some ghetto kid, Sayyon. Lauryn takes good care of you, and you—"

Hearing Lauryn's name made him spaz.

"I'm not a fuckin' kid anymore! I don't need Lauryn to take care of me!" he spat, as he stood.

"Oh, so you your own man, huh?"

"You damn right!"

"Well, act like one then!" she shot back.

He looked at her, shaking his head.

"You just don't get it, do you? . . . I love you. I'll call you later."

He turned and walked out.

"Sayyon!" Bianca called out, but he was already gone—in more ways than one.

* * * * * *

Sayyon took a seat in the booth where Base was waiting for him at Outback Steakhouse. Boonchie sat in the booth directly across from them, clutching a chrome 10-shot .40 caliber under the table. Although Base and Sayyon had done business together before, every meeting was the same, as far as taking security measures. Boonchie was Sayyon's gun, and he never left home without him.

Base set up today's meeting to discuss a matter pertaining to an abundant amount of cocaine at his disposal. This topic first came up a day after Sayyon had purchased the tables and slot machines. Base called Sayyon and asked him if he was interested in the "white girl". A conversation like this couldn't be discussed over the phone, so Sayyon agreed to meet up with him to go into a little more detail.

"I'm glad you could come," Base said, shaking Sayyon's hand as he sat down.

"If it makes dollars, it makes sense," Sayyon remarked, hitting Base with the hood cliche.

Base chuckled.

"Yeah, I like that. I gotta remember it. Listen, we can definitely do big things together, but I don't want to get on your sister's bad side."

"I'll take care of Lauryn," Sayyon assured him.

Base nodded, and then leaned on the table with his arms crossed.

"I've got access to some coke. It's, at best, B-grade but it can be hit once or twice and still be the best product in your neighborhood, and that's something I can guarantee."

Sayyon looked over at Boonchie, motioning him to come and sit in on the conversation. At only eighteen, Sayyon didn't know that much about cocoaine and the prices for it. But nineteen-year-old Boonchie was well versed in the drug game. Plus, if Sayyon brought Boonchie in, he could duck Lauryn's strict policy of not selling drugs: Boonchie would be his go between front man.

"So, what's the price?" Boonchie chimed in after taking a seat in the booth, looking attentively at Base.

"That depends on how much work you can move. I can give you a brick for sixteen-five, if you're buying more than five at a time. Or, I can front you the same work so you won't have to come out of your own pocket. But I would have to charge you eighteen-five, and you've got to move at least five bricks a week."

Boonchie went right into a trance, calculating how much money they could make off each brick, and how he could get rid of five of them in a week.

Sayyon wasn't in his lane, but if the money was right, he was willing to step outside his sister's box for a minute and get at a real dollar. For someone like him, it wouldn't be a problem adapting to the drug life. He was already street, minus the drug dealing.

"I need to see what da product is like first," Boonchie said, coming out of his daze. "If the product is what you say it is and the fiends like it, we can do some business."

Base reached into his pocket, pulled out a small plastic sandwich bag, and passed it across the table. "Here's one ounce. Cook it up to one and one fourth ounces and see how ya fiends like it."

"How much you want for it?" Sayyon asked, looking at the powdery substance in the bag.

"It's free," Base responded. "Just be honest with me when you put this out on the streets. I like you two guys, and I wanna do business with you. Just don't cross me, and I know for sure that I can make the both of you very, very rich."

The white, baldheaded Jew acted as if he was talking from experience. He actually sounded like he could be trusted, and that was the only thing Sayyon really focused on during this entire conversation. He watched Base's body language and firm eye contact and saw sincerity in his eyes. The one thing that Sayyon was good at was judging character, and Base looked like he checked out. For now, it was time to take the work back to the block and see what it could do.

* * * * * *

Spoon sat on the couch in Kiki's living room, listening to the detectives explain how Mark was killed. Spoon was Mark's best friend, and Kiki was Mark's girlfriend. Her cries rang out through the entire house so loudly that it drew the attention of the neighbors sitting outside.

Who the fuck would want to kill Mark? Spoon thought. They didn't have a beef with anyone in the 'hood. *It just don't make sense.*

"We're having a baby!" Kiki cried out. "I'm pregnant! We were having a baby!" She was hysterical.

The detectives couldn't even talk to her to find out any information about Mark. Her sister Margaret had to walk her upstairs away from them. Even with her reaction to the news, the detectives still didn't rule her out as a suspect. Mark's last words indicated that a woman had shot him, and that's what Detective Indira focused on.

"Look, officer. You're gonna have to come back another time," Spoon said, getting up off the couch.

"Yeah, I can see that. But before I go, I want to ask you a question," the detective said as he walked toward the front door.

"Yeah, what's that?"

"How was the relationship between Mark and his girlfriend?" The detective nodded in the direction where Kiki and her sister went.

"Fuck is you asking me that for?" Spoon shot back with an attitude, staring the detective down with hatred in his eyes.

The detective wore a sincere look on his face. "I don't mean any disrespect, but . . ." He hesitated as to whether to give him this information. "Your friend's last words were, 'Dat bitch shot me'."

Spoon looked confused, and from the moment he heard that comment, his mind began to race. He thought about all the bitches Mark was messing around with on the side, and which one of them had the potential to end his life. The only chick crazy enough to do something like that was Kiki, and she was upstairs crying her eyes out. Spoon knew for a fact that she didn't do it. She might act crazy sometimes when it came to Mark, but she wouldn't kill him literally. The only thing for sure was that the streets would be talking, and when they did, he was going to make sure that his ears were wide open.

* * * * * *

The ounce of cocaine was placed inside an empty baby food jar with just enough water in it to allow the coke to cook. Boonchie stood over the stove and put the baby food jar inside of a pot full of boiling water, which caused it to fizz a little before the cocaine turned into a liquid form. Once the oil-like substance dropped to the bottom of the jar, he added the baking soda and stirred it with the back of a spoon. "Give me a little ice," Boonchie instructed Sayyon, who stood by watching the entire process.

Sayyon always heard about dudes cooking coke, but he never actually saw it happen until today.

Boonchie was street for real, and he knew his way around the kitchen a bit, considering that from the age of ten he watched his two older brothers cook cocaine. It was something that he had to learn in order to survive on the mean streets of Philly.

Four crack heads sat at the dining room table waiting as if they were about to be served dinner. They all were in Maxine's house, and if you wanted to get the word out that you had some good new product, this was the place to start. Aunt Jackie, Wayne, Steve and Maxine all sat there cleaning their "straight shooters" out, putting fresh Chore-Boy in them and taking the old stuff out. They even had little makeshift tools they used to make their preparations go faster.

Boonchie came into the room with one fourth of what he had cooked up. He cut it into four pieces, putting a large rock in front of everyone. It was like putting a sheep on a dinner table full of wolves. They were on the product, and before he knew it, all four crack heads stuck glass dicks in their mouths.

Sayyon walked into the room just in time to see a crack head take a blast for the first time. He frowned at the smell of the burning crack, but stood there unfazed, waiting to see the crack head's reaction.

"Talk to me, Max," Boonchie said. He wanted to see what the product was hitting for.

Maxine's face lit up. Her eyes shot wide open like high beams on a car, her mouth started twitching and moving like she had no control over it, and she began rocking from side to side.

Steve's eyes shot wide open also, looking around the room at everything that he thought was moving.

After Aunt Jackie took her blast, she just stared at the pipe as if she didn't know what it was.

Wayne's high beams came on as well, but he took the cake when he stood up, walked right past Boonchie, and stood in the corner looking at the walls.

No one in the room could fix their mouths to say anything. It was as if their jaws locked.

"Oh shit!" Boonchie chuckled, seeing the reaction he was looking for. "Yo, we about to get dis money, my nigga!" he said, looking at Sayyon with dollar signs in his eyes. "Call Base and tell him we need to meet up!"

Chapter 6

Dis shit's fake!" Trinity yelled as she ran into the room with a handful of the money they had taken from Roscoe's van.

Missy was sitting on the couch Indian style and laughing her ass off while watching old episodes of *Sanford and Son.* She was kind of weird like that. Even through the laughter of Aunt Esther calling Fred a 'fish-eyed fool', she heard every word that Trinity yelled. Without taking her eyes off the TV, she stuck her hand out and reached over the back of the couch where Trinity stood. She took the money, glanced at it, and then looked back at the TV. Again, she looked at the money and held it up to the light to see if she could see the bar code line. "What's wrong wit' it? You can see the line in it," she said, turning her attention back to the TV and laughing as Fred kicked Esther out of his house.

Trinity walked over to the table in front of the couch and grabbed a cup of soda. Missy wasn't paying her any attention until Trinity began pouring soda on the money still in Missy's hand.

Shocked, Missy jumped up off the couch, ready to smack the shit out of her. "What da fuck, Trinity!" she yelled out, shaking the soda off the money.

"Look at it!" Trinity demanded after taking the remote control and turning off the TV.

The ink on the money was starting to smear. Neither of the women said a word, but just watched the ink drip off the paper in Missy's hand.

"How much of dis shit is in there?" Missy asked with a blank look on her face.

"I stopped counting at 200K. There's still plenty of it sitting on the bed," Trinity answered, and took a seat on the couch.

"Get Bingo on the phone. Tell him we got his cut, and we'll be there in an hour." Missy tossed the money onto the table and headed for her bedroom.

Bingo was the one who put Missy onto the lick, but he didn't say anything about the money being counterfeit. In fact, he was adamant about getting his cut as soon as the job was done. It was a known fact that he knew every good target for the takedown, but Bingo was also known for playing games too. His only problem was that he was playing games with the wrong chick, and he'd better have a Class-A excuse as to why the ink was fading off the money. If not, he was going to find out first hand why Missy had most of the city shook.

******

If looks could kill, Bingo's throat would have been cut the moment Trinity and Missy walked into the little pawnshop that he owned. The two were looking sexy as ever, and Bingo couldn't help but notice how thick Missy looked in her hip-hugger jeans.

"Ladies! Ladies!" Bingo said, after coming from behind the counter. "Come into the back," he directed, pointing to the small door that led to his small office.

When she walked past him, he felt the urge to palm Trinity's ass because of the way it sat out in a pair of spandex tights. Then he remembered who he was dealing with and thought against it.

"So how did you make out?" he asked, after taking a seat at his desk.

"We cleared about 220K," Missy said, taking a seat in the chair and kicking her Nike Stilettos up onto his desk. "But see we got a problem," she continued, tossing some of the faded money in front of him.

Seeing that, Bingo leaned up on the desk, but at the same time he reached for the 9-millimeter he had strapped under his chair, and placed it on his lap, undetected. Trinity stood there playing with her belly under her T-shirt but Bingo wasn't fooled by her innocent look. He knew exactly what kind of bitches he was dealing with, and he wasn't about to take any chances with them. He took the money with his free hand, looked at it, and then tossed it back on the desk in front of Missy.

"What da fuck is dis, Bingo?" Missy asked with an attitude, removing the Prada sunglasses from her face.

"It's counterfeit money," he replied. "And where's my cut? I told you I get 40% of the take."

Missy jumped up out of her seat and looked at Bingo like he was crazy.

Not only was he admitting to knowing that it was counterfeit, he was also asking for his cut. If she had known that she was going after counterfeit money, she never would have done the job in the first place. She'd risked her life many times before over big scores, but never in a million years would she have done it for that.

"So you did know about the money?" Trinity asked, swiftly drawing the .45 ACP from her waist and pointing it at Bingo before he had a chance to react.

He kept his finger on the trigger, and still felt like he had the advantage, because his gun was pointed toward Missy under the desk.

The look he gave her, along with the sound of a hammer being cocked back made Missy realize the situation she was in. It was exciting to her. This was the kind of shit that turned her on.

"Know about it? Shit, I'm the one who sold him the money!" Bingo said arrogantly.

Missy looked over at Trinity, giving her the eye not to start shooting while Bingo's gun was still pointed at her. Before Missy could say another word, her phone rang, breaking the silence in the room. She wanted to try and diffuse the situation before she even thought about answering the phone. Plus, Trinity was unaware that Bingo had a gun in his hand under the desk. "Look, Bingo. We didn't come here for all this," she said, indicating to Trinity to lower her gun.

Trinity complied, but kept the gun in her hand down at her side.

"Yo!" Missy answered her phone, moving slightly away from the desk where Bingo's gun pointed at her.

"What!" she responded. "Spoon, slow up. What you mean he's dead? What the fuck you talkin' 'bout?" she said over the phone. She quickly glanced back at Bingo but then focused on the phone conversation.

The news was heart-wrenching to Missy, but now wasn't the time to be asking more questions or getting upset. *Mark was my only brother, and someone must have been out of their right mind to kill him*, she thought while suppressing the fury she was holding inside.

Trinity looked over at her and could see that something was wrong, and knew for sure that something was about to happen.

"I'll be there in a few hours," Missy told Spoon. She hung the phone up and turned to face Bingo. She put her phone back into her pocketbook and latched onto the .357 Magnum.

She didn't hesitate squeezing the trigger of the gun in the Prada bag.

The bullet hit Bingo in the top of his left shoulder, causing him to fire his weapon off wildly. His aim was way off due to the bullet wounding the same side of his shoulder as his shooting arm.

Trinity quickly took cover behind a file cabinet, but Missy wasn't that lucky. The last bullet Bingo fired struck her in the thigh. She screamed from behind clenched teeth and pulled her gun completely out of her bag.

Bingo was still sitting in his chair but dropped his gun onto the floor.

Missy slowly limped up to the desk. She pushed everything on the desk to the floor and sat on the desk facing him, so that he was sitting between her legs. She had a crazed look in her eyes, but managed to crack a smile through the burning sensation in her thigh.

"I got money!" Bingo pleaded.

"I know you do," Missy quickly answered. "Where is it?" she asked, waving the gun in his face. "And it better not be counterfeit!"

He nodded toward the wall where Trinity was standing. Behind her was a large picture of a whale on the wall. Trinity knocked it down, revealing a safe.

Missy looked over to see the small pullout safe in the wall. Out of nowhere, she began pumping her fist to play her favorite game of Rock, Paper, Scissors. "We play for your life," she said, playing scissors for the first round without giving Bingo a chance.

"What are you talking about? You can't open the safe without me!" Bingo said, not taking Missy seriously. "You kill me, you won't get the money!"

"This is only the best two out of three," she said, pumping away. "One, two, three!" she said, and played rock.

Bingo didn't say anything, which was a mistake. Missy pointed the gun a mere two-inches from his forehead and pulled the trigger. The close range shot knocked him backward and out of his chair.

Trinity looked at Missy like she was crazy, and shook her head as she reached up and grabbed hold of the small portable safe. "So, what now?" she asked, pulling the small but heavy safe from the wall.

"We gotta go to Philly," Missy said, now thinking only about her brother.

Chapter 7

L auryn sat in the club going over applications turned in by people who wanted access to the gambling room floor. That was the only way anyone could gamble in her establishment. She had a unique system that did away with irresponsible people making her club hot.

The first floor was designated to the public. It had a dance floor, a bar and several touch-screen games. It also included a jukebox and a kitchen that served 20¢ Buffalo wings and potato wedges. Pretty much anyone was allowed on the first floor.

However, most people weren't invited to the second floor. You had to be a member, and all members had to go through a thorough background check—both criminal and a street/'hood background check. No exceptions.

The second floor was flat-lined, meaning there were no walls dividing the rooms, except the bathroom. Up front were two blackjack tables, a craps table in the middle, and seven slot machines in the back. This was the "casino," and it was run just as well as any casino in Atlantic City. In fact, it was a little safer in Lauryn's place than in a legal casino. The only thing missing were hotel rooms, which she had thought about making happen.

Simair walked in just as she was checking one of the applicant's place of employment over the phone. The look on his face prompted her to hang up the phone. He walked over to the bar and grabbed a bottle of vodka from the shelf and two shot glasses. He sat down at the table, poured two shots, and pushed one over to Lauryn, who didn't drink much. She waited for him to say something.

"What's goin' on, bro?" she asked, wanting to get to the bottom of this sit down.

"Our *friend* checked out yesterday," Simair said, holding his shot glass in the air before downing the vodka.

"What are you talking about, Simair?" Lauryn wanted to be sure of what she'd just heard.

"Our friend . . . Mark. He died in the hospital yesterday." The news didn't hit her like Simair thought it would. Although she'd never killed anyone before, she witnessed one or two murders in her lifetime fucking around with her boyfriend, Neno.

Her first and only concern was whether she got away with it. It was broad daylight when she shot Mark, and she wasn't sure if anyone saw her car parked outside of his house. When she thought about it, she took the shot glass off the table and downed the vodka. "You think anybody saw us?" she asked, paranoid about getting caught and going to jail for the rest of her life.

"Man, ain't nobody see us. It was too early in the morning. Plus, the cops would have been up in here. I'll tell you one thing. You better get rid of that dog," Simair advised, thinking about the only evidence that could place her at the scene of the crime.

"I'm not getting rid of the dog. Pebbles is mine now," she shot back, standing firm on her words.

Simair gazed hard at Lauryn and she gazed right back. They were both strong willed, but Lauryn had the edge because she was Big Sis.

"Are you listening to yourself? You're willing to go to jail just because you want to keep the dog?"

She waved him off dismissively.

"No one knows about that. It's plenty of all-white American pit bulls in Philly, Simair."

"Yeah, whateva."

"Whateva is right."

"I just hope you're right," Simair shot back.

"Aren't I always?" she quipped.

Mark's death meant nothing to Lauryn, and it was evident because she went back to going through the applications in front of her on the table. One thing did come to her mind that struck her curiosity. She hadn't seen Sayyon in a couple of days, and that wasn't normal for her baby brother. "Where the hell is Sayyon?" she asked, lifting her head up from the paper.

******

Fifty-fifth and Catherine Street looked like one big fast food joint, except it wasn't the food bringing the heavy flow of traffic to the corner. Cars pulled up and pulled off like a drive-thru. Fiends lined up in the alleyway waiting to get served, and in the middle of it all stood Sayyon and Boonchie.

Base supplied the first five bricks, and Boonchie had calculated paying off the 90K from the first two bricks . . . that is, if they broke them down, cooked them up, and went hand-to-hand selling nicks, dimes, and twenties. That's just what they had decided to do, and Sayyon fell right in line with the drug game. He was like a natural, and from the outside looking in, you couldn't tell that this was his first time.

Boonchie introduced Sayyon to a whole nother' world, and for what it was worth, he had his back through whatever. West Philly was Boonchie's neighborhood, and he pretty much knew everyone in his 'hood. Sayyon was his best, and pretty much his only friend. Despite the fact that Sayyon was a year younger than he was, he respected him like a man. Besides, he knew Sayyon's violent side, and anyone who knew that side of Sayyon knew better than to do anything less than respect him.

Although it was only their second day out on the block, they were doing more numbers than the surrounding strips. The other corner boys' blocks were beginning to slow up. In fact, it made a lot of dudes sick because Boonchie and Sayyon bagged up 700 off each ounce, which made their nickel bags look like everyone else's dime bags. Plus, the product was ten times better. Off each brick, Boonchie turned 36 ounces into 55 ounces, putting the cash value around 39K a brick. Hell, if they wanted to see 90K in a week, this was the only way it was going to get done. If they couldn't see the 90K in a week, Base wasn't going to be able to give it to them at that cheap rate, especially on consignment. If Sayyon and Boonchie could keep this connect, there was no telling how much of the city they could take over.

* * * * * *

It was fight night, and just about everyone on the invite list came to the basement. It was packed, and tonight was Pebbles' debut. She was going up against Izzabel, a tiger-striped pit bull belonging to Fresh Jess, the top dog breeder in the 'hood. Lauryn wasn't too sure about Pebbles, but she was giving out two to one odds, trying to draw as much money as she could. But before the main event took place, two other dogs were already in the ring, scrapping. Spoon was fighting his dog, Bowser against Mike's red nose, Damon.

"So, what does it look like wit' Pebbles?" Lauryn asked Simair at the top of the stairs as they watched the fight.

"If she wins, you'll clear 50K easy," he answered, looking off into the basement at the crowd cheering the dogs on.

Lauryn smiled, hoping that Pebbles would come through.

Will, the pit boss, slid up beside her and whispered in her ear that she was needed on the second floor. Any time someone went on a run on one of the tabletop games, she wanted to be advised immediately.

Lauryn made her way through the first floor to the door that led upstairs. To no surprise, Linda was old school, and if it wasn't her chipping away at the casino's money, it was Ms. Matty, the slot machine fiend. "What's the damage?" Lauryn asked Will as they stood off to the side.

"She's up 11K right now."

"C'mon over here, lil' lady," Linda said to Lauryn. "I know you wanna know how much I won so far," she joked.

"Now, Ms. Linda, I want you to break the house tonight!" Lauryn joked back. "I do want to offer you the opportunity to use the cut-off bar so that you can go home with some money in ya pocket."

"You go ahead and do that, baby. Cut me off at 10K, but I'ma keep gambling though," Linda said, and turned in her chair.

The cut-off bar meant that Lauryn would hold the requested amount in the event that the player went on a losing streak. They wouldn't be able to gamble beyond the cut-off bar. Thus far, no matter what happened, Linda wouldn't be going home with less than 10K. This kind of thing was proven to be good for business, and Lauryn offered it to her faithful gamblers.

"Ms. Linda, you enjoy yourself tonight, and if you need anything at all, you let Will know and he'll get it for you," Lauryn said, before heading back downstairs to the fight.

As soon as she got to the basement, Spoon was already standing in the ring, counting his winnings. The blood was already washed out of the ring, and now the main event was about to go down.

The small room where Lauryn used to keep Lady was now Pebbles' domain. When Lauryn opened the door, Pebbles, along with Lady's seven puppies, spilled out onto the floor. Pebbles knew exactly where the ring was and walked right over to it, jumped over the small wall, and took a seat.

Spoon was stepping out of the ring by the time Pebbles jumped in, but when he turned to get a look at the next fighters, he laid his eyes on Pebbles. He knew every dog that Mark owned, and to be sure before he jumped to any conclusions, he climbed back into the ring and walked up to Pebbles.

Lauryn didn't notice Spoon examining Pebbles because she was too busy trying to put the puppies back into the room.

"Yo, you can't be in the ring wit' the dogs!" Simair told Spoon.

Spoon was tempted to inquire how they got Pebbles in their possession, but he stopped because he might be able to gain more information if he just took a step back.

Fresh Jess put his dog into the ring, and within seconds the fight was on.

Pebbles went right to work, locking onto the lower part of Izzabel's neck and shaking Izzabel all over the ring. Izzabel couldn't get her footing right to save her life, but even then, she managed to take off half of one of Pebbles' ears, being as though that was the only thing she could bite onto.

"Break!" the referee shouted out at the end of three minutes, marking the first round.

GUN SMOKE

Lauryn and Jess quickly jumped into the ring to grab a hold of their dogs. It took a thick stick to pry the dogs' mouths open to separate them. When they did separate, Lauryn tended to Pebbles' ear, so she wouldn't shed any more blood. Izzabel looked like she was out of it, but there were still two rounds to go.

In no time they were back at it, and Pebbles went right back to work, going for the lower part of Izzabel's neck again. Izzabel, though a good fighter, was a little overweight and couldn't defend her neck quickly enough.

"Let's go, baby! Let's go, baby!" Lauryn shouted. "Finish her! Finish her!" she rooted on. She had never been this excited about a dogfight in her life, and neither had Spoon.

Spoon looked on as Pebbles finished Izzabel off the way he knew she would, but it wasn't the actual fight that had him excited. He was excited because he might have found the person who killed his best friend. All he could think about was what the young detective said about Mark's last words. *Dat bitch shot me!* Those words ran through his mind during the entire fight.

As Lauryn cheered Pebbles' victory, Spoon slipped out the basement door, but not before taking one last good look at the joyful Lauryn.

Chapter 8

Blue 2004 Bonneville," Agent Razor announced into the radio, directing his team to stop the car.

Razor and his partner, Toast, left the house they were using to do surveillance on Lauryn's club. The night was their shield in and out of their post, which was only one block over. By the time they got to the blue Bonneville, the cop in the patrol car had already taken Fresh Jess's driver's license and registration.

Jess just sat there in the driver's seat smoking a cigarette, and remained cool, calm, and collected, despite the fact that he had a gun under his seat, a quarter pound of hydro next to his engine, and a half-dead dog in the trunk.

Razor instructed the patrol car to turn off their flashing lights to avoid drawing any attention. Then, instead of walking up to the driver's side window, Razor climbed into the passenger side of Jess' car.

Jess looked over at the suited man in shock. A white man sitting in his car wasn't a good look.

"Jesse Walters from Marshal Street," the agent said. "I'll be honest with you, Jess. I'm a federal agent."

"Yeah? So what do you want with me?" Jess asked, reaching for the door handle like he was about to take off running.

"I wouldn't do that if I were you," Agent Razor advised, seeing Jess's movements. "I've been watching you, and if I wanted to lock you up, I could have done it by now. You have a half-dead dog in ya trunk, and I'm sure whatever you put under your seat when you got into the car can't be anything that's legal. I'm guessing that it's either drugs or a gun. Either way, I can book you if I wanted to."

"So, what you want?" Jess asked, and tossed the cigarette out of the window. "I don't got no info for you, so what could you possibly want from me?"

"I was thinking that maybe you can avoid going to jail tonight and make yourself a few dollars in the process."

******

Linda ended up leaving the blackjack table with a little more than 22K, the most she'd ever won in Lauryn's place. With that much money in her possession, Lauryn had a mandatory policy that Linda would be escorted to her front door by security. Even Atlantic City didn't provide that kind of service.

"Now, Ms. Linda, you make sure you enjoy that money," Lauryn said, happy that Linda, along with a few other people, came out winners tonight. Winning was good for business. It drew people in, and the house always made more than what it lost. The total loss for tonight was around 30K, something Lauryn would make back over the weekend.

Tristian and Shannon, two of Lauryn's henchmen, escorted Ms. Linda to her car, and then followed her down Cumberland Street toward her house. Toughie, Iron, two more of her henchmen, stayed behind with Lauryn and Simair so they could shut the club down for the night.

Lauryn stood on the porch and watched as Linda and her security drove down the street. She noticed the people walking down the street who left the club began scattering, as if trying to get out of the way of something or someone. She looked up and down the street to see what was going on, but couldn't see much on the dark street.

Suddenly, the sound of a pop and a flash drew her attention to the hooded man walking across the street and firing in the direction of the club. Out of nowhere, two more men came from behind one of the parked cars on the block and began firing at the porch.

"Oh shit! Get down!" Toughie and another one of Lauryn's security guards yelled, grabbing her by her collar and pushing her to the ground behind the cemented section of the porch.

Simair was already in the act of squeezing the trigger of his 17-shot Ruger in the direction of the first gunman who turned out to be Spoon. Toughie quickly drew his weapon and began firing back at the other two shooters who were using the parked cars as cover. The night sky lit up with every shot fired.

Dough Boy, another security guard, ran to the door of the club to get outside, but he was met with a barrage of bullets that came crashing through the door. One bullet struck him in his face and sent him to the ground.

* * * * * *

"Shots fired! Shots fired!" the dispatcher yelled over the radio.

This immediately got Agent Razor's attention as he sat in Jess's car.

"Bouvier and Cumberland! Multiple shooters! All units in the vicinity respond with caution!"

GUN SMOKE

When Razor heard "Bouvier and Cumberland Street" his heart almost skipped a beat. He'd just left that street three minutes ago. His adrenaline kicked in, and he tossed Jess's driver's license to him before opening up his door. The patrol car that made the stop was already en route to the scene of the shooting. "I'll be in contact," Razor told Jess before slamming the car door and running to his own car.

******

"Are you hit? Is everybody good?" Simair yelled out to Lauryn and Toughie, who both lay on the porch floor behind a brick pillar.

The gunfire subsided, and all three gunmen fled off into the night, leaving the air full of gun smoke.

Police sirens were getting nearer. Simair knew he couldn't stick around any longer unless he wanted to go to jail.

Lauryn got to her feet and quickly told Simair to get out of here. She knew his situation. Then she ran into the club, damn near tripping over Dough Boy, who was lying on the floor right by the entrance. He was alive and holding the side of his face. "Dough Boy's hit!" she screamed out to Toughie, who was still on the porch.

Simair walked off just in time. Within ten seconds, police cars came from everywhere.

Toughie tucked his gun in his waistband and flagged down the first cop that came down Bouvier Street.

Lauryn continued to yell from the entrance of the club for someone to call an ambulance. "You gonna be good, Dough Boy! Just hold on!" she said, and ran behind the bar to grab some towels to put pressure on his face.

******

Agent Razor drove down Cumberland Street, not stopping to assist the many police officers that were already on the scene. He wanted to avoid anyone seeing his presence on the scene in the event that someone noticed that he was a Fed. If word got out that the Feds were on the scene, it would pretty much be the end of his investigation, hands down. Right now, he was building his case, and knew for sure that this shootout would eventually become a part of it. This was a different ballgame, and when the Feds put a case together, they made sure it stuck.

Razor got on the phone and immediately called Jess. He had an unfinished conversation he needed to wrap up with him. This was how it all started: find the weakest link in the chain, apply plenty of pressure, and see what happens when the link breaks. Normally, that one door will lead to another door, and that door will lead to another, and before you know it, everybody is going to jail.

Although Jess didn't recognize the number on his screen, he answered his phone on the second ring anyway. "Yo!"

"Meet me in Marcus Foster Playground in twenty minutes," Razor instructed before hanging up the phone without waiting for a response.

Chapter 9

Yo, let me holla at you," Sayyon told Boonchie as he pulled up to the corner. Traffic was still moving and the block was starting to pick up, but not enough to see 90K in the next four days. If they were going to depend on getting it done from this corner alone, it wasn't going to happen. Sayyon didn't want to lose out on having a good connect, and within three days of being a drug dealer, he had a vision. People had already been asking him if they could buy weight from him, and he hated the fact that he had to tell them no.

"What's good, bro?" Boonchie acknowledged him and jumped into the truck.

"Yo, where we at wit' dis money?" Sayyon inquired as he looked out of the window at the constant flow of fiends coming through the block. He was beginning to feel himself and the lead position as 'the boss' was kicking in.

Boonchie could see the change in his attitude, but he was cool with it just as long as Sayyon didn't look down on him like he was some type of peon. He knew exactly how Sayyon was feeling, because he was the same way when he got into the drug game. It was the feeling of having money, power, and respect—a deadly combination if you didn't know how to control it. "Yeah, I can see ya concern," Boonchie said. He already knew where Sayyon was going with his question. "Da block's doin' numbers, but we're just now hittin' the 20K mark."

Sayyon let out a sigh. Twenty grand in three days was all right for starters, and maybe in a few weeks the block could do 20K a day, but right now it was time to turn it up a bit. It was time to expand. They had a deadline to meet, and by all means Sayyon was going to meet it. "Yo, from now on, anybody who wants to buy some weight, you call my phone. I want you to keep pumpin' the block wit' 24/7 shifts. Hire some workers if you have to. I'm about to go down my way and go hard as a muthafucka," he explained to Boonchie, taking the leadership role.

"You goin' down to North Philly?" Boonchie asked with a concerned look on his face. "What about ya sista? Hell, what about ya brotha?"

"Dog, I'm all in right now, so I'll cross that bridge when I get there. Right now, I'm tryin' to get dis money, ya dig?"

Hustling down North Philly would definitely cause problems within the family, but at this point it really didn't matter. Sayyon had gotten a taste of some money, the kind of money he wasn't seeing running errands for his sister. It made him feel like he was the one in charge and he was getting addicted to the feeling.

******

Lauryn sat in the hospital waiting room, waiting to see Dough Boy, who had been shot in his left cheek. The bullet shattered his cheekbone and then exited near the top of his nose. He had been in surgery all night, and Lauryn wasn't going to leave the hospital until she knew that he was going to be all right.

It was no surprise that the detectives had asked her and Toughie a million and one questions, but they gave them the same answers as everyone else did who was there: "Three men just walked up and started shooting at the club." That was the story that pretty much everybody gave. Toughie also admitted to firing back at the gunmen. Since he was a legal security guard with a license to carry a firearm, he was released from the police station after the detectives recovered ballistic evidence from his gun.

The hospital was packed. This was odd, considering it was 3:30 in the morning on a Thursday.

The doctor came into the waiting room and explained to Lauryn what was going on, and allowed her to visit with Dough Boy for a moment before he was to undergo another surgery.

As she walked past the rooms on her way to see him, she caught something unusual in her peripheral vision that piqued her curiosity, and she decided to be a little nosy. There was a woman in one of the rooms stuffing all kinds of things into her pocketbook. From the way the woman opened up every cabinet, it looked as though she was stealing. Then, right before Lauryn walked off, the woman turned and caught Lauryn staring at her. They held eye contact for a split second before the doctor called Lauryn to tell her that Dough Boy was in Room 114.

* * * * * *

Lauryn pulled up on Gratz Street, and the only person standing outside jumped on his phone. He would know that black Range Rover anywhere.

Two minutes later, Sayyon emerged from one of the houses and made his way to the truck. Lauryn could see "drug dealer" written all over him by the way he looked. He wasn't fresh to death like he always was. The signs of fatigue were all over his face. Sayyon looked like he hadn't slept in days. He walked across the street and jumped into the truck, bringing the strong aroma of purple haze in along with him. Lauryn didn't say anything. She just looked out of her window at the fiends running in and out of the same house that Sayyon had just left. She felt a sense of disappointment and didn't even want to ask the questions she already knew the answers to.

"What's goin' on, LaLa?" Sayyon said, calling Lauryn by her nickname instead of Big Sis like he normally did.

"I haven't seen you in almost a week. Yeah. What is going on? And why do you smell like weed?" she snapped.

"I've been busy," he replied in a calm manner, also looking at the heavy traffic going in and out of the house.

She turned to look at him and became sickened at how much he looked like their father, sitting there like he was the boss of all bosses. Sayyon looked as though he had the whole world in the palm of his hands. He looked at his ringing phone but didn't answer it. It had been ringing ever since he got in the car. "Sayyon, I hope—"

"LaLa, I'm not the same person that I was a week ago. Hell, I'm not the same young bull I was a couple of years ago!" he said, cutting her off. "If you couldn't tell by now, I'm a man, Big Sis, and I got to start doing what's best for me."

"You sound really stupid! You think selling drugs is what's best for you?"

"You sound like a hypocrite!" Sayyon shot back. "What's the difference between me selling drugs and you running a dogfighting ring? What's the difference between me selling drugs and you running an illegal casino? Nothing!" he shouted. "How long did you expect me to be out here in these streets and not become a product of my environment?" For the first time in a long time, Sayyon watched as a few tears dropped from Lauryn's eyes.

She felt guilty and partially responsible for her baby brother taking this course in his life. He was right. She sounded like a hypocrite. How could she try and keep him out of the streets when she, herself was knee deep in it?

"Yo, don't do dat," Sayyon said, reaching over to wipe the tears from her cheeks. "You act like I just told you that I was a faggot or something!" he joked, trying to get her to smile.

She did smile, but only at his corny comment. This was a tough pill for her to swallow, but at the same time, she had to respect the fact that her little brother was finding his own way in life. All she could do at this point was make sure that he wasn't being used and abused. The streets could get ugly at any time, and she knew this firsthand from being with Neno. "So, do you need some money or anything?" she asked as she wiped the tears from her face.

He laughed a little and thought about the amount of work he was moving. "Naw, Big Sis. Ya lil' bro ain't fallin' short. If I do anything, it's always gonna be big."

"Oh yeah? Well, pay for that truck I bought you!" she said, talking about the Caddy.

"See me in about two weeks!" he shot back, and opened the door to get out.

She quickly grabbed his arm, reminding him that this conversation was going to resume at a later time. She was definitely going to get the intel on who, what, when, where, and how he was getting his work. Telling him about the shooting at the club had crossed her mind, but she decided not to tell him because there weren't many people in the 'hood that knew he was her brother. He was pretty much out of harm's way, which was exactly where she wanted him to be, because if he found out that somebody shot at his sister, he would turn North Philly upside down.

Chapter 10

T rinity walked into the diner on 22nd and Lehigh with serious hunger pangs. Missy stayed in the car, drowsy from a mixture of penicillin and pain pills that she stole from the hospital the other night. Everything smelled so good, and with a pocket full of twenties, Trinity wanted to order everything. She just had to keep all liquids away from the counterfeit money.

"Can I help you, sweetie?" Ms. Beverly asked, turning away from the grill and attending to Trinity.

"Yeah. I'll have everything that man has on his plate times two," Trinity requested as she pointed to a handsome young man who was demolishing the large plate of sausages, eggs, potatoes, and a side of flapjacks. "Damn! Slow down! Ya food ain't goin' nowhere!" she commented, taking a seat on the stool next to him.

Simair lifted his head to see Trinity sitting there, looking like something that just came out of a fashion magazine. He felt a little embarrassed and didn't know what to say to her. Her beauty had suppressed his hunger momentarily, causing him to lower his fork and wipe his mouth off with a napkin. "You're not from around here, are you?" he managed to get out.

"Why do you say that?"

"Well. First, ya accent is different. It sounds like you're from somewhere in New York."

Her accent was obvious. Born and raised in the Bronx made it hard to sound any different.

"Plus, I know pretty much everybody down in the badlands, and I never saw anything down there that looks like you." He complimented her. "You gotta be like Colombian or something, right?"

Trinity smiled. It was hard not to. Not only was Simair cute, but he had a way with words. Even a quiet, sexy killa like her could use a few compliments in her life. After all, she was still a woman. Messing around with Missy all day, every day didn't quite afford her the opportunity to have much of a social life. It was always business. "I'm Dominican," she said, quickly correcting him. "And my name is Trinity." She stuck her hand out for a shake.

"My name is Simair," he replied, taking her small, soft hand into his. *Damn, that's crazy!* he thought.

"Is that for here, or to go?" Ms. Beverly butted in, breaking the eye contact they shared.

"You should stay and have breakfast wit' me." Simair threw that out there before Trinity could answer Ms. Beverly.

"I can't," she reluctantly answered. She regretted bringing Missy along. "I have somebody waiting on me."

Before Simair could say another word, his phone rang. He looked down at it to see that Lauryn was calling. It was good that this phone call came through, because for a moment he had forgotten all about the beef that was going on. "Yo, what's good?" he answered, after getting up and excusing himself to Trinity.

"Meet me at the club in about an hour," Lauryn told him as she was pulling away from Susquehanna and Gratz Street after talking to Sayyon.

"Say no more," he replied, and hung up the phone and returned to his seat. To his surprise, Trinity was gone. He looked around the diner to see if she had taken a seat somewhere else, but she was nowhere in sight. He even looked out of the window to see whether he could catch her walking down the street, and again nothing. Just that quickly, something so beautiful ran in and out of his life without leaving a trace!

"Here you go, baby," Ms. Beverly said, sliding a small piece of paper across the countertop. "She left this for you. It's the digits," she said with a laugh. "Now, don't get your young ass turned out, messin' wit' that Cuban stuff!"

"She's Dominican, Ms. Bev. She's Dominican." He chuckled as he made his way out the door.

* * * * * *

Mr. George came down the steps from his bedroom with his bathrobe and house shoes on. He was ready to go out for yet another one of his journeys into the world. It was scary, because it was as if he was sleep walking once he left the house, and there was no telling where he would go. That's why Lauryn always found herself picking him up from odd places.

When Mr. George opened the front door, he was shocked to see Missy standing there with a gun in her hand. She pushed him back into the house and closed the door behind her. Mr. George backed all the way up to the couch and fell into it with fear in his eyes. Missy pointed the gun at him, which caused him to flinch and brace himself for the possibility of being shot.

"Do you know who I am?" Missy asked as she squatted down in front of him with the gun still pointed in his direction.

"N-n-no, I don't know you. Why are you in my house?" Mr. George stuttered. He had no idea who Missy was and why she was in his house. He was scared for every bit of two minutes before he got up enough courage to reach out for the gun as fast as his old bones would let him, which wasn't fast at all.

Missy moved the gun from out of his reach, and then smacked him across the face with it.

Mr. George quickly got some "act right" and sat back on the couch with his hands where Missy could see them.

"I wanna play a game. Do you wanna play a game?" Missy asked him, and switched the gun to her left hand, so that she could use her good hand. "If you lose, you die. You win, you live," she said, and began pumping her fist for Rock, Paper, Scissors. "One, two, three!" she called out, and played scissors on her first go.

Surprisingly, Mr. George pumped his fist too, and played rock for his first round and won.

Missy smiled and so did Mr. George. "Best two out of three," she reminded him, and pumped her fist for round two.

Mr. George pumped his fist too, and played paper for the second round, while Missy played scissors, which tied the score.

"One, two, three!" she announced, and played rock for the third round.

Mr. George played paper, and placed his hand over Missy's, and smiled at the fact that he had won.

This was the first time that Missy had lost at her own game, and for a second it made her want to shoot Mr. George for that reason alone. But she kept her word, letting him live. She stood up and backed up to the door with her gun still pointed at him. He just sat on the couch with the same crazy smile on his face as he watched her open the door. "Stay in the house, old man!" she commanded before leaving the premises.

Chapter 11

L auryn pulled up in front of the club, where she was met by Simair, Toughie, Tristian and Shannon. She walked right past everyone without saying a word, and went straight into the club.

The damage inside wasn't that bad. . . . that is, without having to step over the large puddle of blood on the floor in front of the door. A few broken liquor bottles behind the bar, several bullet holes through the front door and front window, and a bunch of trash lying all over the place was the total of the damage.

"Everybody take a seat," Lauryn said, after cleaning off one of the tables by the kitchen. "It's obvious that we have a problem, but one thing I can't allow is for this problem to shut down the club. Tristian, I want you to go down to Home Depot and get a new front door and window. Shannon, I want you to fill the bar back up with liquor, and clean Dough Boy's blood up. Toughie, I need you to go around and promote an open bar and free food for tomorrow night. Let everybody know that the club is back open."

"What about the situation?" Tristian asked, looking to get in some gunplay.

"Don't worry about dat. I'ma take care of it. I really don't need y'all runnin' around shooting up everything movin' and making the neighborhood hot. It wouldn't be good for business." She was playing it smart. She wanted to minimize the possibility of a war jumping off that could get a lot of people killed or hurt. Her conscience was messing with her already due to Dough Boy being in the hospital because of something that she had done. She wanted to handle Spoon on her own in the most discreet way possible, and she didn't want any witnesses or accomplices.

"Simair, I need to have a word wit' you," she said, getting up from the table after dismissing everyone else. "I want you to get my black book, call my high rollers, and tell them there's a $100 free play tomorrow night. I need you to step up and run the casino for me for the next few days while I take care of this other business."

Simair just looked at her like she was crazy. He had no doubt that she was capable of putting in her own work, but he'd be damned if he sat back and let her do it at all, let alone by herself. He wasn't going for it, and there would be no negotiating either. "You must be out ya rabbit ass mind if you think that I'ma let you move out by ya'self! You might be older than me by a couple of years, but you're not the boss of me, Lauryn!" He looked her in the eyes, so she could see the conviction behind his words. "Spoon shot at my sista. So when I catch him, I'ma shoot him in his face, and there's nothing you or anybody can do about it!"

Lauryn took in a deep breath, and knew how serious he was. And in a sense, she didn't expect anything less. When it came to bustin' a gun, Simair did it at an all-time high, and everybody in the 'hood knew that . . . even Spoon.

Lauryn felt the same way Simair did, and even though she didn't have anything to prove by going out and putting the work in by herself; she still felt obligated to do it, considering someone had tried to take her life.

But to be honest, with her it was a little deeper. It seemed that after she found out that she caught her first body, she felt like killing was easy. She was kind of turned out by the whole "take a life when I want to" syndrome.

One thing was for sure. There was no question as to whether Spoon was going to die. It was more so of who was going to kill him first: Lauryn, the silent killer, or Simair, the type that killed on sight no matter where he was. Neither of them was even worried about the other two gunmen Spoon had with him. They both figured that if you cut the head off, the body wouldn't function.

* * * * * *

Missy looked down at Spoon, angry that his dick was almost too big for her to sit on. But she fiercely took it all in, thrusting her hips back and forth on top of him. She'd only been riding him for about five minutes and had already come once, and was now working on number two. Her breasts bounced with each motion, and her face bore signs of both pain and pleasure. The more she stroked back and forth, the wetter her pussy got.

Spoon could feel her juices dripping off his balls, and every time he reached up to feel her perfectly round D-cup breasts, she slapped his hands down. "You better not cum!" she demanded, wanting him to stay hard for the duration.

Her lips were so juicy and glossy that Spoon couldn't even look up at her without thinking about how good they would feel wrapped around his dick. Her body was immaculate, and had he continued to look at her, it would have only made him cum faster. Missy wasn't making it any easier, reaching back and spreading the bottom of her ass cheeks apart so that his dick went in just a little deeper. He could damn near feel his balls going inside of her. She growled, feeling herself about to cum again.

"Oh, shit!" Spoon exclaimed, feeling her walls tighten around his dick and the fluids gushing around.

"You better not cum!" she demanded again. She was still not done with her sexcapades. She jumped up off him, and a suction cup-like sound pierced the room. "Beat dis pussy up!" she told him, and got in the doggy style position with a vicious arch in her back.

Her ass was so fat that Spoon damn near burst before he got a chance to get his dick into her. He got behind her and slid every bit of nine inches inside, and wasted no time in punishing her with long, hard, deep strokes.

Missy held onto the headboard and looked back at his eight-pack abs. She threw her ass back at him to let him know that she could take it. She couldn't help but reach beneath herself to play with her clit at the same time.

"You better not cum!" Spoon demanded, palming both of her ass cheeks. He then sped up his strokes to the point where it became a pounding.

* * * * * *

Trinity was sitting downstairs, bored by the entertainment. Chink, who was one of the other shooters at the club, sat there and smoked blunt after blunt, something Trinity wasn't into. Chink wasn't even attractive to her, and it seemed he was more into the weed than anything else. The sound of Missy upstairs getting her back blown out was the most intriguing thing happening in the house.

Trinity was saved by a phone call. She rifled through her pocketbook and finally pulled out her cell phone. The number on the screen was unfamiliar. "Who's calling?" she answered as she got up from the couch and went into the other room.

"You had me a little worried, the way you left without saying anything," Simair said into the phone as he drove down 23rd Street.

Trinity grinned, actually happy that he called. She unintentionally thought about him ever since leaving the breakfast spot. He was the cutest person she saw in Philly thus far, and if there was anyone she was going to holler at before she left the city, it was going to be him. "I'm sorry, but I told you that I had somebody waiting on me," she replied as she looked off into the cloudy room that Chink was sitting in.

"Well, look. I was wondering if I could pick you up later, and maybe we can get something to eat. By the looks of the food you ordered this morning, I know that you can get your chow on!" he joked.

"That sounds good. The only thing with that is I'ma have to call you later and let you know what time I'll be available. I have a lot of running around to do all day, and I'm not sure when I'll be done."

"Well, whenever you're free, make sure you give me a call, Ms. Busy Body!" he joked as he pulled over and parked on Diamond Street.

Trinity had no idea that Simair was sitting outside about a block away, waiting for Spoon to surface. Specifically, Spoon's last known address was the same one that she was occupying that very moment. Simair was trying to get the job done before Lauryn had a chance to put herself out there. If he had to, he would sit out there all day and night. By the looks of the way he had his car in the cut, that's exactly what he planned to do.

* * * * * *

Missy sure had a weird way of grieving after a loss. The sex with Spoon was really just another way to relieve her stress. Spoon was like her boy-toy whenever she came to Philly to chill with her brother, Mark, and whenever Mark brought Spoon to New York, the same rules applied. It wasn't often that she came to Philly. In fact, she hated Philly even though she was born there. Her short history in the city left a scar on her psyche. She felt like she had been dragged through the mud at an early age. The only good thing that remained there was her baby brother.

Spoon sat on the edge of the bed, smoking a blunt while Missy was getting dressed. He explained everything there was to know about her brother's murder, and why he felt Lauryn had something to do with it. He told her about the entire setup Lauryn had with the club/casino/dogfighting operation. He also told her about the shooting that Chink, Roach, and he did last night on the club.

"How the hell is she running a casino?" Missy inquired, seeing dollar signs as she always did.

"Yeah, she's running a mini Atlantic City on the second floor, complete with tables and slot machines," Spoon responded before getting up to get dressed.

"How much money do you think she's pulling in with the casino?"

"I'm not sure, but I know it's damn good numbers. Shit, I lost a couple of grand there myself." He cocked back the 9-millimeter and tucked it into his back pocket.

Missy's intention when she came to Philly was to attend her brother's funeral, kill the person who murdered him, and then return to New York. But now things were starting to change. The only thing that could hold her attention—other than counting money—was taking money. Her mind was racing like a greyhound.

"So, what are you thinking about?" Spoon questioned, curious as to why she was staring out of the window.

"I need to get into the club, so I can see for myself before I make any determination as to whether or not I'm just gonna kill her, or rob her and then kill her. I think I'm entitled to some compensation," Missy said as she looked at the ice cream truck as it passed by the house.

"Well, I can't get in, because I just got finished shooting at them, but . . ."

"But what?" She turned her attention to him.

"I think I know a way I can get you into the building. Just tell me that you know something about pit bulls."

Chapter 12

Sayyon pulled up and parked on the corner of 54th Street, around the corner from the strip, leaving his chick, Bianca, in the passenger side of his truck. He didn't want to draw any attention to himself, being as though he was trying to sneak up on the block to see how it was running when he wasn't around. It wasn't that he didn't trust Boonchie with the work, because he did, but rather it was more so the fact that Sayyon was rising to another level in the streets at an alarming rate.

Today was the day that Sayyon was supposed to meet up with Base to discuss further business. That is, if Sayyon could come up with the 90K by eight tonight. It was a good thing that he decided to sell some weight, because that was the only thing that made him an extra 40K in two and a half days. Whatever Boonchie had from the block was going to put him over the hump and right where he needed to be.

As expected, the block was moving like crazy. Just about everybody was outside, and it was more traffic than ever running up and down the block. Crack heads zoomed past Sayyon like they were in a marathon. He expected Boonchie to be in the middle of it all, but unfortunately he wasn't. Sayyon couldn't see him anywhere in sight, and for a second it irritated him. At this stage in the game, Boonchie needed to be on top of every dollar that passed through this corner at all times. From a distance, he could see the few flaws the corner had that needed to be fixed immediately before it turned into a hazard.

"Yo, where's Boonchie?" Sayyon asked one of the workers, as he made his way through the crowd of fiends.

That question and whom it was coming from took Tay by surprise. But what was more surprising was that nobody was around to watch Tay's back as he served numerous customers. Anybody could have walked up on him and robbed him, or better yet, the cops could have locked him up without even breaking a sweat. This was the kind of shit that irritated Sayyon.

"Oh shit, Yon. What's good wit' you?" Tay shot back with a smile, lifting his head from the crowd. "Boonchie ain't come out yet. I thought he was wit' you."

"So who's out here watchin' ya back?" Sayyon asked, looking around.

"Aw man. I'm good out here," Tay said, lifting his shirt to show him the 9-millimeter on his hip.

Frustrated, Sayyon scratched the top of his head, holding a curious look on his face. "Shut dis shit down," he told Tay, grabbing his arm and pulling him up from the ground.

Tay didn't realize what Sayyon was telling him to do until he saw the anger in his eyes and heard the conviction in his voice. Fiend after fiend kept coming down the block, and Tay could do nothing but let them walk up, be denied, and then turn them away. Sayyon didn't have to say another word. He turned away and headed back to his truck.

As soon as he got into the truck, Bianca noticed the anger in his eyes. "What's wrong, babe?" she asked, turning to face him.

"Nothin'," he answered, grabbing his cell phone from the center console in an attempt to call Boonchie.

Bianca was beginning to worry about him. She loved him with all her heart. They were high school sweethearts, and both of them had aspirations to go to college together and leave the hood. The recent opportunity that presented itself made Sayyon put those dreams on hold for a moment. With a lot of young males in the city of Philadelphia, the dope game always made a nigga detour from his goals. No matter what the situation was, Bianca was going to ride with her dude in whatever he was going to do, just as long as Sayyon understood that by the end of the summer she was going to college with or without him.

* * * * * *

Simair was on his way back to the club when his phone started ringing. Looking down at the display, he noticed that it was Trinity, a person he didn't mind talking to. Especially since he wasted hours sitting outside of Spoon's crib waiting for him to come out. The countless police cars that kept coming down his block drove Simair away, for now.

"Is this really her? The busiest person in the world," Simair joked, answering the phone.

"Oh, you got jokes." Trinity chuckled.

"I can't lie. I feel honored that you called."

"Yeah. Well, you told me to call you when I get some free time, and now I got some. I was thinking that you could meet me somewhere."

Trinity needed to find some time to get out of the house that she'd been cooped up in for the past twenty-four hours. Missy was still lying in bed with Spoon, and it didn't look like she was coming out of the room any time soon. Sitting in the house with Chink was definitely out of the question. If Missy needed her, all she had to do was call Trinity on her phone. She was somewhat familiar with the city, since she used to come down to visit family when she was younger, so there was no need to worry about getting lost.

"You name it," Simair said, thinking about how beautiful she looked.

"You know where Outback Steakhouse is at over Southwest?"

"Do I," he replied sarcastically. "I can be there in thirty minutes." Simair looked into his rearview mirror at the cop that just pulled up behind him.

Outback Steakhouse was one of the few places Trinity knew about in the city. Truth be told, if she had asked Simair to meet her on the moon, he would have found a way to get there. Bad bitches were hard to come by in the city, and Simair was a little pressed to bag her before somebody else grabbed her attention. She was pretty as all out doors, and although he was cocky in his swag, he knew he had to bring his A-game fucking with this Dominican dime piece. She was so distracting, and Samair was so caught up in wanting to see her, he almost forgot that it was fight night in the club. Nothing was more important than securing his sister's money, but tonight he was going to have to find a way to have his cake and eat it too. All within the next four hours when the first fight would start.

* * * * * *

Lauryn sat behind the craps table looking on as Black from West Philly threw the dice toward the back of the wall. He had been hitting numbers all night, and the only thing saving Lauryn from going broke was the fact that Black wasn't betting a lot of money. Even still, the people around him were also betting. So all of them together were starting to make a dent in Lauryn's pockets. It was nothing major, but enough to hold her attention for a moment. But not for long. Whatever money was lost on the craps table would be made up on the blackjack table, or with the dogfights later on that night. That was the beauty of owning a casino. The house always won more than it lost, no matter what.

GUN SMOKE

The sound of a slot machine going off quickly caught Lauryn's attention. When she walked to the back, she saw the penny slot machine flashing and blinking its lights. To no surprise, old-man Jimmy was sitting in front of the winning machine with a huge smile on his face. This was the second time this month he hit a jackpot, and this time it was for five thousand dollars. Last time, he hit for three thousand dollars on the nickel slots.

"I got you again, lil' lady," Jimmy said, rubbing the side of the machine. "One day I'ma hit you for the big one," he joked, looking over at the dollar slot machine sitting in the corner.

The jackpot was up to seventy-five thousand, a nice piece of change for somebody in the hood. The problem with the dollar machine was that nobody ever hit it. Ever since the day Lauryn brought it through the doors ten months ago, the machine never sounded off. It had gotten old real fast, and the only time anybody ever played it is around the first or the fifteenth of the month when people got an extra few dollars to try their luck. But as long as people played the game, the progressive would grow, and as long as it continued to grow, the people would play it.

"Mr. Jimmy, I'ma have to put you on slot machine restriction if you keep this up," Lauryn joked, signaling one of the pit bosses to come over and pay him.

Lauryn could feel her cell phone vibrating in her back pocket. When she pulled it out, the screen showed a blocked number. It could only mean one person was calling under these circumstances.

"Hey, babe," she answered, walking away from the noisy slot machine.

"Hey, beautiful. What's goin' on?" Neno asked, his voice sounding as sexy as ever to Lauryn.

"Nothing but work, work, work. I swear I can't wait for you to come home, so I can fall back and get some me time," Lauryn said, looking off into the other room at Black throwing dice across the table.

"Yeah. Well, that won't be much longer." Neno chuckled.

"I know. How much longer do I got till that day comes?" she asked, damn near ready to cry. She missed him so much and wanted him home.

The phone got quiet, and for a second, Lauryn could hear somebody in the background saying something to Neno. She had no idea what was about to happen next. As she listened closely, her heart damn near dropped to her stomach. "Next stop, Philadelphia." Lauryn heard the announcement being made over the loudspeaker. She looked down at her phone again to make sure she wasn't tripping. Thinking about it, she never heard the prison operator say anything when she first answered the phone. Lauryn put the phone back to her ear.

"So, are you goin' to stand there with ya ear to the phone, or are you going to come pick me up?" Neno chuckled, waiting for Lauryn's reaction.

She screamed, happy as hell to hear those words coming from Neno. She didn't expect him to be released so fast. He just received his green sheet from the parole board, and was waiting for a bed in the halfway house. It was a shock, but nevertheless, Lauryn made her way over to the pit boss, letting him know she was leaving out for a moment. From there, she went down the steps and out the front door en route to pick up her man.

* * * * * *

"Why do you look at me like that", Trinity asked, twirling the alfredo noodles around her fork and trying her best to avoid eye contact.

78

Simair was pleasing to Trinity's eyes. Light brown-skinned, black, thick wavy hair and an athletic body. He was always cool, calm, and collective and every time he spoke, his voice was soothing. His raw honesty was a plus, something Trinity had never experienced from any of her past boyfriends.

"If I told you, you probably wouldn't believe me."

"Well, I think you should try, because it's starting to get a little weird," she joked.

Trinity couldn't stop blushing. Simair stared at her as if he was looking at a goddess. She never had this much attention paid to her, ever, and sitting in front of Simair made her feel different. Trinity could act and be treated like a lady instead of playing the gangsta role all the time. This was her chance to show her sensitive side, and to Trinity it felt good to be looked at the way Simair was looking at her.

"What if I told you that I never seen anybody who looks as beautiful as you do. When I look at you I see . . ." Simair just sat there, not touching anything on his plate. He really wasn't hungry at all, but rather enjoyed just being in Trinity's presence.

"What do you see?" Trinity asked.

Simair wanted to be honest with her by answering her question, but he didn't know how she was going to take it if he told her the truth about what he was thinking. Being as though they'd just met, he didn't want to blow it and scare her off on their first official date. But Trinity wasn't going to let it go. She was interested in what he had to say.

"What do you see?" she asked again, wanting him to answer the question.

"I see my future," he replied, looking Trinity in her eyes with the puppy dog face. "I see me doing everything in my power not to miss this opportunity of making you my girl."

"Who said that this was an opportunity?" she asked, sitting up in her chair with a curious look on her face.

"The opportunity presented itself the morning I met you in the diner. And being as though we made it this far tells me that I still have a chance," he answered, not taking his eyes off her.

Trinity couldn't help but blush even harder. For a moment she thought that he was about to say something stupid or crazy, but him seeing her as his future was more than a compliment to her. Not only was Simair cute, but he had a way of keeping her attention, something most men couldn't do. Trinity smiled from ear to ear, hoping that Simair wasn't just spitting game.

"See that right there," he asked, pointing at her smile. "I want to be the one who makes you do that every day."

His comment only made her smile wider. *If he doing all this for a shot of pussy, all he had to was ask*, she thought.

Simair's ringing phone interrupted their conversation. Lauryn had a special ring tone, so he knew exactly who it was. He excused himself before pulling the phone from his hip and answering it.

"What's good, sis?"

"Nothing. I need you to get back to the club. Neno just came home, and I'm going to pick him up from the train station right now," she said.

"Oh yeah? Neno Patino came home, huh?" he said, happy for his sister. "Well. Look, I'm on—" Simair stopped mid sentence, and the reason had just walked through the front door of the restaurant. Seeing Roach, one of the men who shot at him and Lauryn, walk in with a female was like having an orgasm. His heart began to race. He slipped the phone from his ear and back onto his waist without saying another word to Lauryn.

Trinity could see the change in his behavior and wondered what in the hell was going on. She looked around to see whatever Simair was looking at, but didn't notice anything out of the way.

"We gotta go," Simair said, pulling out a wad of money and placing a few twenties on the table.

"Why? What's wrong?" Trinity asked, still looking around the room.

Simair wasn't trying to avoid Roach, but rather wanted the confrontation to happen outside where there weren't many witnesses. Trinity didn't say another word, following right behind Simair out the front door. Although the beef was on site, Simair had to play it smart, so he wouldn't end up going to jail fucking around with Roach.

Roach, on the other hand, didn't even notice Simair in the building, nor did he notice Simair and Trinity getting up and leaving the restaurant. Roach, of all people, should've known that when a nigga got beef in the streets, he had to stay on point at all times, wherever he was at.

Chapter 13

It was a moment Lauryn had been waiting for ever since the day the police put Neno into the backseat of the patrol car four years ago. She stood inside the 30th Street station waiting at terminal six. The train was pulling up, and the anticipation of seeing him grew. Tears flowed down her face, and she hadn't even seen him yet. Just knowing that he was coming was more than enough. It wasn't long before she could see Neno coming up the escalator with a small box in his hand. She ran to him as if he were a soldier who had just come home from war. Running right into his arms, that first kiss on land meant the most to an incarcerated thug. For a moment it seemed as if nobody else was in the train station as Neno wrapped his arms around Lauryn and kissed her ever so softly.

"I missed you," Lauryn managed to utter, holding on to his muscular arms.

Letting his arms slide down the center of her back, he could feel the butt of a gun near her ass. It shocked the shit out of him, mainly because his first instinct was that he was out on parole. He pulled back from Lauryn's kisses and gave her a curious look, wondering why in the hell his girl had a gun on her. She really didn't realize it until she saw the look in his eyes, and then she remembered.

"What's that all about?" Neno asked with a slight attitude, tapping the butt of the gun.

Carrying a gun was natural for Lauryn, especially since the recent drama that had been going on in the hood with

Spoon. Lauryn had to put Neno up on the ongoing beef and much more before he actually hit the streets. Before he left, Lauryn wasn't doing anything but being his girl. Now, she was like a boss in her own way, and aside from all the bodies Neno had under his belt, Lauryn had put in just as much work as Neno did when he was out there in the streets.

A lot had changed while Neno was in jail. He heard a few things about Lauryn making moves, but every time he asked Lauryn about it during the visits, she would always downplay what she was doing. She did that for the purpose of not wanting to stress him out while he was bidding. Either way, he was satisfied with her accomplishments and how far she had come in the last four years, but for her to have a gun on her like she was in the Wild Wild West, sparked a concern.

"Oh, that's a story in itself. We got plenty of time to talk about that, but for now let's just go home for a few hours before I take you to the halfway house," she said, guiding her hand down the center of his chest, and ending in grabbing a handful of his dick.

* * * * * *

Simair and Trinity sat in the car in the parking lot in total silence. Trinity still didn't know what was going on with Simair, or what, if anything was about to happen. What she did do was keep her hand by her pocketbook just in case she had to grab her gun. She got straight out of feminine mode and right back on some gangsta shit quick, hoping it wouldn't have to be Simair she'd be shooting.

Before Trinity could say anything, Roach and his female friend came strolling out of the restaurant holding hands. Simair locked in on them like a hawk, and it finally hit Trinity that Roach was the reason for all the tension in the air. Looking a little closer, she recognized Roach from somewhere, but couldn't put her finger on it. The only people she'd actually met since she'd been back in the city was Chink and Spoon. Roach wasn't really around that much, but she'd seen him before. That was the reason she recognized him.

"Stay in the car," Simair said, breaking the silence.

He reached under his seat and grabbed the Glock .40, checking to make sure he had a bullet in the chamber. Trinity raised her eyebrows in shock, watching as the whole situation was about to unfold. She had to admit he looked even cuter when he was mad, and it kind of turned Trinity on seeing this side of him. She just sat back and watched as he got out of the car and was about to put in work.

* * * * * *

"We're going back to my place or yours?" Roach asked his lady, Precious, before turning on the interior light.

"Yours," she responded with a seductive look as she watched Roach take his gun from under the seat and put it in the center console.

She didn't even get a chance to say another word before Simair walked up to the driver side window where Roach sat. All he saw was a shadow, and without warning, Simair rapidly opened fire into the car. Every bullet struck Roach in the chest and face. Simair stuck his hand further in the car in order to hit Roach at a closer range, knocking holes in his face the size of quarters.

Precious screamed at the top of her lungs, only seeing the flashes from the gun with every shot. Nothing but gun smoke filled the inside of the car, damn near choking her.

Simair's hand jerked and jerked after every shot until his clip was empty. It wasn't until he ran out of bullets that he realized he was about to leave behind a witness. Regretfully, he started to walk away from the car knowing that he didn't have much time before the people in the restaurant started looking out the window to see what was going on.

Precious finally got her wits together and reached for Roach's gun in the center console. She was scared to death and didn't want to die. Simair walked around to the passenger side of the car, just to give her a stern threat before going back to his car, but when he got there he was met by gunfire. Precious wildly fired out the passenger window out of fear.

Simair dipped off just in time, dodging several bullets that damn near hit him in the face. She didn't have any aim, but she was squeezing the hell out of the 9-millimeter in his direction. She was so focused on trying to hit Simair, she didn't even see Trinity walking up on the driver side of the car with her gun down by her side. Trinity stuck her gun into the window, unfazed by Roach's dead body, and fired a single shot to the side of Precious's head, killing her instantly.

Simair peeked up from behind the parked car he dipped behind to see Trinity waving at him to get back to the car. He did, climbing from behind the car and walking past the passenger side of Roach's car seeing Precious's head slumped over the dashboard.

Simair couldn't help but stare at Trinity sitting in the driver seat as he slowly walked back to his car, somewhat shocked. Confusion was an understatement. When he finally did get into the car, Trinity gave him a look with a sinister grin behind it. He couldn't believe what had just happened and why it happened. *What the hell was Trinity doing with a gun? And better yet why would she risk having a homicide on her shoulders for a man she barely knew?* Simair thought. Questions about Trinity ran a triathlon inside his head while he sat in the passenger seat as Trinity made her getaway.

One way or another, whenever the car stopped again, Simair was going to get some answers.

Sayyon and Boonchie pulled into the Small Storage Company on Main Street where they were supposed to meet up with Base. Sayyon finally caught up with Boonchie and got the rest of the money. That is, all except a couple grand, in which Sayyon had to borrow from one of his workers. The conversation in the car was kept at a minimum during the drive up there. Boonchie was high off syrup, pills, and weed. Sayyon just looked over at Boonchie in disgust as he stopped the truck right in front of Base's black Aston Martin Vantage. Even though only Base and two other men waited there, they were still heavily armed.

"Yo, get up. We here," Sayyon said, backhanding Boonchie's arm, waking him out of his sleep.

He woke up, but Sayyon could tell he was still high as shit. That getting high shit was a big turn off for Sayyon, and this was one of the many reasons why. If shit hit the fan right now, and Base decided to rob or kill Sayyon, Boonchie would be of no use. Even bringing him to this deal was kind of embarrassing, and before Boonchie had a chance to make a mockery of Sayyon, action needed to be taken.

"Yo, stay in the car," he instructed Boonchie, turning and grabbing the black bag full of money out of the backseat.

"Why? What's up?" Boonchie asked, barely keeping his eyes open.

"Just stay in the car!" Sayyon shot back with an attitude.

Boonchie tried to put up a small protest, but Sayyon wasn't having it, warning him sternly not to get out of the car. Boonchie just sat there and looked at Sayyon through bloodshot eyes. Sayyon returned the stare, pulled a gun from under his thigh and tossed it onto Boonchie's lap before exiting the truck. Boonchie did as told, but of course with an attitude. Even though he was high, he still didn't like the way Sayyon was talking to him.

"Got damn, big homie. What's good wit' you?" Sayyon said, extending his hand to Base as he walked up to him. "I hope you didn't think I was bullshittin'." Sayyon wore a serious look on his face, placing the money on top of the hood of the Aston Martin.

Base smiled. He liked Sayyon. Always did. It was kind of surprising that Sayyon moved over ninety thousand dollars in product in a week. He didn't expect it coming from someone who didn't even know shit about selling drugs a week ago. Base could see the talent in Sayyon, and that's just what he'd been looking for to really get his paws dug into the city of Philly. Having the whole Jersey on smash was good, but having just the city of Philadelphia was even better.

"I didn't doubt you for a second," Base said, walking him around to the back of his car. "In fact, I got something special for you." He winked and popped open the trunk.

At first sight, the inside of the trunk looked empty, but Sayyon knew better. With a latch lifted here and a few buttons pushed there, the whole floor panel lifted up. Base had enough work to supply the whole tri-state area. Sayyon had never seen that many bricks of cocaine in his life, and he didn't have a clue what he was going to do if Base was dropping this much shit on him. But after a few seconds, hunger pangs started settling in, and Sayyon had a vision.

"This will be the last time I front you cocaine. From now on when you come, come spending your own money," Base said, removing several bricks and placing them in a trash bag. "Can you handle ten birds?" he asked.

"Given the opportunity, I can handle everything you got in this trunk," Sayyon replied with conviction.

Base stopped bagging up the coke and looked up at Sayyon, who was looking back down at him. For some reason he believed every word Sayyon just said. But with it being so early in the game, he wasn't willing to take the chance of finding out if he could move the fifty bricks sitting in his trunk. Base had to admit, the offer was tempting.

"Well, in time we'll see how true that statement really is," Base said, closing the secret compartment and then the trunk. "Here's ten bricks. Same price applies. I'm not putting no specific time limit on the money, but I do like surprises. Call me when you're ready." Base extended the bag and his hand for a shake.

Sayyon agreed, taking the bag and shaking Base's hand. Before he got back to his car, he had already calculated the money and how long it would take him to move the product. He had the mentality of a hustler and the brain of a genius. Once he set a goal, no matter what it was, he always reached it.

Once he got back in the truck, his joy faded away at the sight of Boonchie nodding off like he'd just shot his arm full of dope. He was better off having Bianca with him right now. As Sayyon thought about it, that wouldn't have been a bad idea. It was inevitable, but as soon as Boonchie sobered up, Sayyon was going to check him about his bad habits. Right now, he really had to focus on driving safely, so he could successfully get the work back to the crib without getting pulled over.

* * * * * *

Chapter 14

One, you were about to get shot the hell up. Even I could smell her fear from where I was sitting. She was bound to get lucky the way she was blasting. Two, you're just a genuine dude. And three . . . I feel something when I'm with you. It's kinda . . . different. Didn't want nothin' to happen to you," Trinity answered Simair with a shrug when he asked why she had killed for him.

"The gun though. You always carry—" Simair said, but was cut off.

"Oh yeah!" Trinity said matter of factly.

Simair nodded once. "All right. So . . . It is what it is. Let's go to my spot for a while. I need to check out a few things."

"Okay. I'm wit' it."

Thirty minutes later, Simair walked into the club and was quickly reminded by Shannon that it was fight night. He damn near forgot with all that just went on, but was led straight to the basement where the dogfighters were. Trinity just followed behind Simair, clueless as to what was going on, or where she was. The place was jam packed too. People were lined up against the wall, eager to fight their dogs.

"Yo, I didn't know the faces of the normal fighters, so I just let everybody with a dog come in. I didn't want to draw any attention with them standing outside. Bystanders are still outside waiting to get in," Shannon informed Simair as he walked down the steps.

"What's going on?" Trinity asked Simair over all the barking as they walked into the basement.

"Fight night," he yelled over the loud room.

Simair got order in the basement by banging a mallet against a wooden table. Everybody got quiet, even the dogs, while Simair explained the rules and regulations of the ring for any new fighters. Pebbles was the main event, so whoever wanted to go up against her had to be the one betting the most money. Up until then it was a couple good fights and a lot of money to be made.

In minutes, dogs were in the ring and the fights were on. Fresh Jess was the first one in the ring with his new dog, Whitey, and it looked like he was back for revenge for what happened to his last dog, Izzabel. She was going up against Nate's dog, Roscoe. During the fight, Trinity looked around the room, taking in the whole atmosphere and soaked in all the excitement. To her surprise, she locked eyes with Missy who stood against the wall next to a pit bull. She started to walk over to her, but didn't once Missy shook her head no. She didn't want anybody to know that they knew each other right away.

After several fights, it was time for the main event, and the new reigning champion, Pebbles, was taking on any challengers, male or female. Simair walked to the back of the basement, opening up the door to where she and the puppies were housed. The room was silent as she made her way to the ring without having to be on a leash. Missy quickly noticed Pebbles from the pictures Spoon gave her. She even kept one of the photos of Mark and Pebbles with her, and when she pulled it out it was a positive match. Pebbles looked healthy and well rested. Once she stepped foot in the ring, the bidding for a fight began.

"I got five grand on my dog," Reds yelled out from the crowd.

Some of the bystanders burst out laughing at how much Reds was trying to bet. Everybody in the building knew that main event fights started at no less than fifteen thousand. Even Simair had to laugh at the number.

"All right, is anybody serious?" Simair shouted, still chuckling at Reds.

"I got fifteen thousand."

"I got eighteen thousand."

"Twenty thousand over here."

The bets just started coming out of nowhere, and the higher they got the better. That's what the main event was all about. It was no limit to how much you could bet. The house would take on any bet as long as the money was on the wood.

"I got fifty thousand," a female voice from the back of the room yelled out.

That number stopped all other fighters from yelling out any further. Niggas had confidence in their dogs, but fifty thousand was a little too high for the average city dogfighter.

Missy walked up to the ring, tossing a stack of money to Simair. He took one good look at the money, and then back at Missy before locking in the bet. He didn't even know who she was, but with fifty grand on the line, it really didn't matter. Hell, Simair didn't even notice that the money was counterfeit, and that was after he checked a couple bills while he counted the money out. Just as long as he kept it away from water, Missy was in the clear. In the event he did catch on to the money, Missy had plan B in effect, consisting of a vicious shootout.

Baby, the Hennessy colored female dog Missy came with went straight to work on Pebbles. Spoon picked Baby because he knew that Baby was the only other dog in Mark's kennel that could beat Pebbles. Hell, it wasn't too many dogs on the east coast that could beat Baby, and what she was doing to Pebbles in the ring was proof of that. Pebbles was trying, locking on to Baby's lower neck, but what Baby did next was never seen by anybody. Once Missy saw the opportunity Spoon told her about, she went for it.

"Weezle, Baby. Weezle!" Missy yelled out.

Baby unlocked her jaws from Pebbles neck, turned and bit down on Pebbles' nose. When Pebbles let go to get a better hold of Baby, Baby somehow locked onto her snout and lower jaw, pinning her mouth shut. Like a pair of vice grips Baby clamped down, not shaking nor growling, but rather suffocating Pebbles slowly. Everybody looked in amazement as Pebbles tried to come from out of the hold, but the more she struggled, the less oxygen she was getting to her brain.

Simair was even impressed with the way Baby was going to work, seeing that it was no way Pebbles was coming out of this hold. Nobody had ever seen a dog kill in this fashion, and within a couple minutes, Pebbles had checked out from lack of air and oxygen. The crowd in the room went crazy. Hearing all the oooohs and ahhhhs, Missy soaked it all up. It was exhilarating.

"That's called Fight Night!" Simair leaned over and shouted into Trinity's ear over the loud crowd. Then he escorted Missy and Baby upstairs, so she could be paid.

Chapter 15

Mrs. Lincoln, how are you today?" Agent Razor asked, coming into the small room where the little old lady and her husband sat.

Mrs. Lincoln went to the local detective a couple of days ago telling them that she had some information on Mark's murder. She and her husband lived a couple doors down from Mark. Mrs. Lincoln heard the shot and saw a female and a male leaving Mark's house the morning he was murdered. She got the first two numbers of the license plate of the car they jumped in when they left. Although she didn't know what kind of car it was, she knew the car was blue. Mrs. Lincoln was sure that if she saw the male again she could positively ID him, being as though she got a better look at him than she did of the female.

Agent Razor took down her statement, the two numbers of the license plate, and all her contact information before ending the interview. If this was the work of Lauryn, Agent Razor was definitely going for the RICO Act once she was indicted. He was on Lauryn's ass, and decided to make her his own little project. He wasn't going to rush the process and bust her right away for the dogfights that went on in the basement, but with patience, he knew that it was much more to this young lady than what his eyes could see thus far. His gut instinct told him that she was bigger than what the local cops thought she was. Right now, it was time to get the hell out of the office. Later on today, he was supposed to meet up with Jess to see what new info he had.

******

Neno wasn't going to be able to come outside of the halfway house today, so Lauryn took the opportunity to check up on her grandpop. When she got to the house, the front door was wide open. Lauryn just knew that he probably wasn't home, and more than likely he went off on one of his expeditions again. This time she was wrong. Walking into the house, she saw him sitting on the couch in nothing but his bathrobe.

"Oh shit!" she mumbled, seeing a pan on the stove in flames.

Thick smoke wafted from the kitchen where he had left some eggs on the stove. Lauryn quickly ran into the kitchen and turned the stove off, throwing the burning frying pan into the sink of water. Had she not been there, the whole house would have caught fire. Mr. George just sat on the couch watching TV like nothing was going on.

"Pop-Pop, you know you left the stove on?" Lauryn said, kneeling in front of him.

"Oh, oh, oh, Pumpkin. I'll turn it off in a minute," he said, not taking his eyes off the TV.

Lauryn then noticed the black ring around his eye. It looked kind of fresh, and she was curious as to how it got there.

"Pop-Pop, what happened to your eye?"

He turned and looked at her, stuck his hand out and began pumping his fist. He wanted to play Paper, Rock, Scissors, or at least that's what Lauryn thought. She felt so bad for him. Lauryn knew it was time for him to go into a nursing home. There, he could be watched all day, and Lauryn wouldn't have to worry that much about him knowing someone was at least watching him. Until then, he was going to have to come live with her before he ended up hurting himself, or even worse, killing himself.

******

Sayyon opened up a couple new blocks down North Philly that were as critical to him moving work at a fast rate. Hancock and Cambria was the most lucrative, especially since it was once known to be a million dollar corner back in the day. His old head, Raw, was the previous owner of the block, but due to his incarceration it was pretty much open to the best man. Sayyon took a page from his book and put double-sealed dime bags on the corner, attracting fiends from everywhere. They were called double-sealed bags because it was so much crack inside the first bag, he had to put the first bag into another one. Plus, it was his signature product. Fiends knew that when they were copping double-sealed bags from that corner, it was like getting a value pack. Off the break, Sayyon took five of the bricks, cooked up 55 ounces off each brick, bagged up $750 off each ounce and made five bundles out of each ounce at $150 a bundle. With 275 bundles in a brick, he brought back a little more than $40,000. Multiply that by five and Sayyon was at the 200 grand mark. In the first twenty-four hours, the block was moving 50 bundles, and within forty-eight hours it was up to 75 bundles easy, and still growing. He estimated having Base's money by the end of the week, and roughly rounded off spending 200 grand of his own with another week's worth of hustling. Sayyon was turning it up, and he had made a little crew over night. It consisted of a few young cats from around that way that he knew. They were hungry and willing to go the distance for the block, especially since Sayyon was looking out for them.

Boonchie was still working with the remaining three bricks from the last flip. Catherine Street was doing good numbers, but North Philly was always known for getting more money than West Philly. Even though Sayyon told Boonchie to do the same thing he was doing with the coke, Boonchie was doing his own thing, cooking up 60 ounces off a brick and bagging up $1,000 an ounce. The coke was good enough to take that kind of hit and still keep its potency, but it wasn't moving as fast as it could be. Boonchie was just being greedy, and everybody knows what greed gets you: dead or in jail.

******

"The detective on ya brother's case said they have a witness who saw two people coming from your brother's backyard the morning he was killed," Spoon told Missy, who still lay in the bed, ass naked.

That caught her attention fast, forcing her to sit up and listen attentively. Up until now, she was starting to forget about the real reason she was back in the city. She was so caught up with other things, that the pursuit for her brother's killer slipped her mind for a moment. Other personal issues came rushing back to her at once, the minute she got back to the city. Unsurprisingly, the whole little dogfighting set up that Lauryn had intrigued Missy. And once Simair introduced her to the second floor, she saw nothing but dollar signs. She even blew twenty-five grand from the fifty she won on the blackjack table. It was a good thing Spoon was there to remind her where her focus should be. He, of all people knew the influence the city had on people, and if one wasn't careful, they could turn a short visit into a permanent stay.

"You know who the witness is?" she asked, reaching over and grabbing her phone off the nightstand.

"He said it was some old lady that lived a couple houses down from him. I don't have a name, but I think I got an idea of who she is."

The first person he thought about was the old lady who always complained about the dogs barking and sometimes getting loose. It really didn't matter because Spoon already made up his mind about who was behind it. The only reason he'd been hesitating getting at Lauryn was because he'd heard that Neno was home. It wasn't a single soul in North Philly that didn't know who Neno was, and how much work he'd put in.

"I hope you ain't come out here faking," Spoon said, grabbing his gun off the dresser and placing it into his back pocket.

"You better watch who da fuck you talking to, Spoon. I don't do no fuckin' faking, nigga."

"Yeah, I can't tell," he shot back.

"Don't take your fuckin' da shit out of me as a sign of weakness. You got a nice shot, but we can definitely get some understanding about who I am in the event you forgot," Missy threatened, sliding her hand under the blanket and grabbing a hold of her gun.

Spoon just looked at her and smiled. He really didn't want no problems, knowing exactly the kind of bitch Missy really was. He knew that Missy didn't have a problem bustin' her gun. That was one of the things he secretly loved about her. Hurting her would be the last thing he would do. He walked over to her, leaned in, and kissed her pouted lips with a smile on his face.

"Get dressed, Missy, or we'll be late for the funeral," he said.

Missy had forgotten, and she felt a little embarrassed by it. She quickly dialed Trinity's number. She hadn't seen her since the fight night and didn't really get a chance to holler at her about how she managed to get in the club. Missy had a reality check. It was time to blow the spot, but before that happened, Missy had a couple issues to deal with.

"Hello," Trinity answered, sounding like she just woke up.

"Yo, get up. You know it's my brother's funeral today."

"All right," she grunted into the phone.

"Get up!" Missy shouted.

"I'm up. I'll be there in a minute." Trinity hung up the phone and looked back at Simair, who was putting long dick into her back.

******

Simair palmed Trinity's ass cheeks, shoving every bit of ten inches of dick inside her. The strokes were slow, long, and deep. The way he tapped up against her back wall made it hard to control the sensation of cumming all over his dick multiple times within minutes. She swore she could feel him in her stomach, and without a condom in play, it only made the sex more personal.

"Turn over," Simair demanded. He pulled his dick out of her before he came and placed her on her back.

His dick was rock hard, shiny, and wet from Trinity's pussy juice. It even had a sweet smell to it, which made Trinity want to reach down, get a finger full of herself and put it in her own mouth. Seeing that almost made Simair cum. He climbed on top of her and slid his dick back inside of her warm womb. At the same time, he leaned down and pressed his lips against hers. He watched her make all kinds of funny faces from the pleasure he was giving her. Slowly, he inched his manhood in and out of her, growling slightly in pleasure from her warm, wet walls closing in on his dick. She passionately kissed Simair back, stuffing her tongue inside his mouth and allowing him to suck on it as if he wanted to swallow it.

Trinity moaned with every stroke. The deeper he went inside her, the more she could feel the tension building up inside of him. It was to the point where she could feel his dick throbbing. At that very moment they both locked eyes. She felt the thick, warm cum filling her pussy. Simair was about to pull out, but Trinity palmed his ass cheeks and pushed him back inside of her.

"Give me all of it," she whispered into his ear, swaying her hips side to side as she felt her orgasm coming on.

Simair continued to stroke deeply and at her pace, accepting her tongue as she inserted it back into his mouth. If Trinity didn't know any better, it seemed as if Simair was making love to her. For what it was worth, she felt like she was doing the same thing.

"Oohh, papi. I'm cummin'," she cried softly into his ear, wrapping her arms around his back.

Simair could feel every bit of her pleasure pouring onto his dick. Instead of pulling out, he just lifted her leg, turned her on her side, and lay behind her with his dick still inside her. They lay in Simair's bed, marinating in each other's juices, and if it wasn't for the recent phone call, Trinity would have went straight to sleep. Simair, on the other hand, did take the opportunity to get a few winks. During that time, Trinity crept out of the bed, got dressed, and made her way to Spoon's house to pick up Missy for the funeral, with a big smile on her face.

She was sleeping with the enemy and loving every minute of it.

Chapter 16

I t cost a nice penny, but his safety was worth it. Lauryn sat in her grandfather's house packing up a few of his belongings to take to her house. She found a nursing home suitable to put him in, but the interview was about a week away.

As she rambled through a couple boxes in the basement, she ran across a couple photo albums. Looking through it, she could see a lot of pictures of her grandpop. More obvious were the many pictures of a little girl he was holding. Lauryn realized more pictures of the little girl filled the album than anybody, and that's when Lauryn pieced together that it must have been her mother. Deeper into the album, George took pictures with two other teenage girls, who Lauryn figured were her aunts who weren't fathered by George but were raised by him. She compared her mother's pictures to the pictures George had of her in another album. She smiled at the thought of how much she resembled her mother, and wondered how she looked before she died.

Looking deeper into the box, she found an ultra sound picture, a pair of baby shoes, some custody papers, and her original birth certificate. Lauryn really didn't know much about her mother except what her father told her and what little she could get out of George. Hell, she really didn't know much about anybody in her family except her grandpop. Growing up, she never got the chance to meet most of her family, including her aunts and uncles. They were already grown and out on their own by the time Lauryn came to live with him. She didn't even know where her mother was buried. Sitting in the basement going through the boxes made her want to learn more about the woman who gave birth to her. She just didn't know she already knew more than enough.

******

Missy sat across the street and watched as a young woman took a few boxes out of George's house. She wondered what connection she had to the old man, and more importantly, where old man George was at. Missy was more upset that George didn't show up at Mark's funeral since Mark was his youngest son. That's one of the many reasons why she hated the old man—that and other hateful family secrets. He never seemed to care about his family. Missy started to go over to the woman and say something, but decided to just follow her to see if she would lead her to George.

******

Sayyon pulled up to 55th Street looking for Boonchie. Tay was sitting outside serving the many fiends that walked up on the block. Directly across the street was the biggest crap game going on. Weed smoke was all in the air. Boonchie sat in the middle of the block posted up talking to a couple hood chicks, high as he wanted to be. He didn't even notice all the attention the loud crowd was causing by sitting on the corner and shooting dice. This was bad for business, and at this point Sayyon was fed up.

"Got damn, playboy. Let me holla at you," Sayyon told Boonchie, cutting off his conversation.

Boonchie walked off from the females and followed Sayyon up the street. Boonchie was Sayyon's right hand man, but when it came down to getting money, that friendship shit was placed on the back burner and business was put first. Boonchie was a little reckless with how he was running the block, and Sayyon couldn't afford to take any losses, or even worse, start being looked at by the authorities.

"Yo, you don't see all these muhfuckas on the corner gambling?" Sayyon asked, pointing down the street.

"Yeah. Dat shit ain't about nothin'," Boonchie replied, brushing Sayyon off.

"Dis a fuckin' business, Boonch. We in it to get dis money, not to be sitting around getting high all day and fuckin' wit' dese dirty ass hood bitches. All these muhfuckas out here ain't good for business. You tryna get locked up?" he asked, raising his voice a little.

"Dis my shit. I run dis shit down here. You run North Philly. As long as the money right at the end of the day you shouldn't be complainin'," Boonchie snapped back.

He felt like he had the right to do whatever he wanted since this was his hood. Sayyon was two seconds away from smacking the shit out of Boonchie. He sounded so ungrateful, and for a second it sounded like he wanted to do his own thing. To Sayyon it seemed like a good idea, because if he kept fucking with Boonchie, this shit wasn't going to last. It probably would be best for them to split up for now before it was too late. Sayyon was on a mission, and Boonchie wasn't acting like he was hungry. He let the few grand get to his head.

"Look, you keep what you got and I'll keep what I got. I'll pay Base what we owe him, and you can do ya own thing. When you ready to flip let me know," Sayyon suggested.

Boonchie nodded his head and gave Sayyon a sarcastic smile as if he was relieved. He felt like Sayyon was somewhat looking down on him like he was the boss. The weed smoke and pills clouded his head. He couldn't see that Sayyon was just trying to put them in a better position. There was no boss between the two of them, and up until now, every dime they made was split straight down the middle. Boonchie didn't see it because he was spending money just as fast as he made it. Sayyon was still learning the drug game, but he knew all about stacking money, and that was half of the drug game in itself. Boonchie, thinking that he was one up in the game accepted Sayyon's suggestion. "Dis nigga is gettin' soft", Boonchie mumbled to himself as he walked off.

He was under the impression that he was getting over on Sayyon, but little did he know it was the other way around. Sayyon might have been new to the game, but he knew how to count money. Boonchie wouldn't last a week before he was broke again. If Sayyon didn't know anything he knew that a fool and his money are soon parted.

Chapter 17

How much is there?" Missy asked, walking back into the room where Trinity was counting the money.

"It's still over two hundred thousand here. I think when you was gambling you was using the real money instead of this," she answered.

Missy came up with the idea to move over two hundred thousand dollars in counterfeit money in Lauryn's club. Considering the fact that Trinity was good with Simair, she would be able to move some of the money too. Killing Lauryn was the next priority, and then after that it was about time to make a speedy, but profitable exit.

Trinity just sat there confused, not knowing what to do because she was actually starting to feel Simair. She didn't want to possibly ruin things between them by moving counterfeit money through a place where he worked. She also knew that if Missy got caught, she was liable to do anything, and that meant shooting any and everybody that got in her way when she attempted to exit the building.

But there was other key information Trinity didn't have. Vital information like knowing that Lauryn was Simair's only sister. This was something she definitely needed to know and consider before going through with Missy's plan, because if she thought for one second Simair wouldn't put a bullet in-between her eyes for the sake of his sister and that casino, she was sadly mistaken.

******

GUN SMOKE

In the middle of the day, Boonchie stood outside counting some money he just got from one of his workers. High like always, he sat on an abandoned porch, unaware of the black Ford Taurus creeping up the street. Once he finally picked his head up and saw the vehicle, he knew for sure that it was the jump-outs, aka the police. He didn't have any drugs on him, but a large .45 Millennium was sitting in his car about twenty yards up the street.

As soon as the car approached Boonchie, the thought of running set in his mind, but after thinking it through, he really didn't have a reason to run. The car stopped, and Boonchie waited for the occupants to get out. Oddly, the car just sat there. Boonchie stood up, and that's when all four doors opened. Out jumped four black men, dressed unlike any police officers Boonchie had ever seen. All four men carried guns, and by the time Boonchie realized that it wasn't the cops, it was too late.

"Run and I'ma blow ya fuckin' head off," the passenger said, holding a Mack-11 in his hands.

"Whoa! What's all this for?" Boonchie asked, sticking his hands in the air.

In broad daylight, these niggas weren't playing any games. Had Boonchie decided to run, it would have sealed his fate. As they walked up to Boonchie, he looked down the street to see if one of his young workers was on point, but they weren't. Tay was too busy standing in the middle of a crowd of fiends, and the lookouts were messing around with a few chicks that were passing by.

While the passenger held Boonchie at gunpoint, another guy walked over to him and patted him down. Boonchie thought this was going to be a basic robbery, but it turned out to be more. After getting searched, the guy led Boonchie to the car. He wasn't trying to be kidnapped and felt that once he got in the car it was a wrap. For a moment he hesitated, putting up a short struggle, but a single shot to his knee urged him to comply immediately. They threw him into the backseat. Then all four men got back into the car, and the driver pulled off just as calmly as he pulled up.

******

Agent Razor snapped photo after photo of Lauryn, Dough Boy, and whoever else walked in and out of the club. He noticed some renovating going on in the house next door to the club. Lauryn would often walk in and out of that house as well. The top windows had mirror tint, so Razor couldn't see inside the second floor, nor could he get any good pictures. It ate at him to want to know what was going on up there. After talking to Jess and getting a couple dogfights captured on his cell phone, Razor had enough to get a warrant, but not enough evidence to get the kind of conviction he was looking for. Jess was supposed to do some gambling in the next couple of nights, so that might be everything he was looking for. The photos were also going to be beneficial for identifying all the players involved in the whole operation. That, along with getting Mrs. Lincoln to point out the guy she saw coming out of Mark's house on the morning he was killed.

"Smile beautiful," Agent Razor said, snapping his final pictures of the day.

******

Lauryn sat in the back of the club looking at the DVD of Fight Night and how Baby killed Pebbles. She was impressed by the fight and how Baby worked. She actually remembered seeing the dog somewhere before, and for some reason Mark's backyard came to mind. She could have sworn she saw Baby in one of the cages when she was leaving with

Pebbles. With that type of performance, she wasn't mad about losing fifty thousand.

Looking up from the TV, Lauryn could hear from the laughing and horse playing, that Simair was coming into the club. He had a little extra glow on his face that Lauryn hadn't seen in a while. She knew it had to be a girl, because that's the only thing that could make him smile like that. Lauryn didn't dig into his personal life much, but today she just couldn't help herself.

"Who is she and where is she from?" Lauryn asked, nudging his arm.

He smiled even harder thinking about how good the sex was. He tried to avoid the question, but Lauryn wasn't going for it. "Spit it out, nigga, wit' ya whipped ass," she joked.

"She's Dominican. Good girl and she go hard," he said, thinking about the situation at the restaurant.

"So when can I meet her?" Lauryn picked up the remote control and rewound the fight.

"Soon. Let me make sure she's the one first."

"Speaking of the one. Who in the hell is this one?" Lauryn pointed at Missy's image on the TV. "She looks new."

"Yeah. She said her name was Dynasty or some shit like that. She ended up losing half of what she won at the blackjack table the same night," he told Lauryn, trying to loosen up the blow of losing the fight.

She squinted at the TV screen, pausing the DVD to get a better look at Missy. Feeling like she recognized her from somewhere, she just stared at her. The girl looked familiar as hell, but when she couldn't put it together, she turned off the TV.

"I gotta go pick Neno up from the halfway house. I was supposed to be taking him to meet Sayyon today for the first time," Lauryn said.

Sayyon really didn't know who Neno was. At the time Neno and Lauryn were dating Sayyon lived out West Philly with his Mom. By the time he moved down North Philly, Neno was already in jail. Lauryn talked about him from time to time, but not enough for any memories to stick.

"So how long can he stay out for?" Simair asked, hoping he could get a few minutes to chop it up with him.

"For good. That's why I need you to hold the club down for the rest of the week so I can spend some quality time with my boo."

A big ass smile framed her face. Lauryn thought about all the back breaking sex she was about to have for the next few days.

"Look at you. You talking about somebody being open. But I'ma hold you down with the club, big sis," he said, nudging her back on the arm.

******

Boonchie got caught slippin', and when he did, he lost just about everything. He was more than happy that he made it out of the situation alive. Normally, in situations like kidnapping, the victim always ended up being killed after they got the money. They did however, beat the living shit out of Boonchie. As he sat in the hospital, he couldn't stop his mind from wandering off into stupid land. The math wasn't adding up, and he took every possibility into consideration. But at the end of the day, the only person he could come up with was Sayyon. He probably didn't do it physically, but Boonchie had a feeling that he had something to do with it. The kidnappers knew too much info about him. They didn't even have to ask where his stash house was at, pulling right up to it on the first shot. That was too much of a coincidence.

Just as his thoughts continued to ramble, Sayyon came walking into the emergency room. He had his hat cocked low, but took it off once he reached Boonchie's room.

"Fuck is goin' on, dog?" he asked, pointing at Boonchie's knee.

"How you know I was here?" Boonchie asked with a curious look on his face.

"Ya girl called me and told me what was going on. What da fuck happened?"

"I got 'napped. The niggas took everything, dog," Boonchie said, struggling to sit up in the bed.

"What you mean they took everything?" Sayyon asked with an attitude.

"Everything. The money and the work."

"You know who it was?" Sayyon asked with a serious look on his face.

Boonchie, however, thought that Sayyon was looking suspicious. Still a little traumatized by the whole ordeal, his paranoia made him consider everybody as a possible suspect, even Sayyon. He didn't make a fuss about it, but rather just lay back in his bed.

"Naw, dog. I don't know who it was." He chuckled, resting his head on the pillow. "But I'll be all right," Boonchie said, pretty much dismissing Sayyon, who felt the vibe from Boonchie's attitude.

"Yeah. Well, if you need something let me know." Sayyon backed up and left out of the room.

Boonchie watched Sayyon leave, wondering if his best friend had become his enemy.

******

Lauryn finally got Neno to a place called home. Her business was only in Philly, but she rested her head in a different place, still in Pennsylvania, but about two hours away from the club. When they pulled into the driveway, Neno couldn't believe how big the house was. It was a beautiful four bedroom, three and a half bathroom home sitting on two acres of land.

"Damn. Dis where you live?" he asked in astonishment, getting out the car.

"No, babe. This is where *we* live," she answered, pulling the extra set of keys out her pocketbook and handing them over to Neno.

The plush master suite furnished with a king-sized bed with a fish tank over top of the headboard and a double walk-in closet was the first room Lauryn took him to. A hot tub and a swimming pool had been installed in the backyard.

"Oh, you doin' big things," Neno said, coming from out of the large bathroom decorated with his and hers sinks and a walk-in shower.

"Naw not yet, but as soon as you get ya ass in this bed, I will be," she said with a seductive look as she started to undress.

Everything he wanted to know could be talked about in the morning. The quickie in the hotel the first night he came home was nothing. Right now, Lauryn had something to get off her chest, and she was going to need Neno's full, undivided attention. Now that he was officially home, Neno could take his time and show Lauryn's body all the attention it yearned for over the past four years. When Lauryn went to turn the lights out, Neno declined.

"Leave them on. I gotta see everything," he said, climbing onto the bed.

Lauryn eyed him seductively and replied, "Everything?"

"Exactly."

Lauryn did a slow strip tease, enticing Neno as she pulled off her shirt and bra, revealing her large juicy breasts. He was all over her, taking her hard nipples into his mouth, one at a time. "You just don't know how much I've been dreaming about you in my cell, yo," he remarked.

Lauryn's head tilted back as she replied, "Show me how much, baby."

Neno laid her down, and instead of taking off her skirt, he just pulled it up and slid off her panties. His ten-inch dick stood at full attention as he gripped the base and pushed it inside her wet, juicy pussy.

"Sssss, ohh, baby, wait. It's been a while," Lauryn protested passionately, as her pussy stretched to accommodate his size.

But his lust wouldn't let him wait. Her pussy felt so good gripping his dick like a glove. She cocked her legs up on his waist and Neno began to grind her hard and deep, in a stir-it-up motion that made Lauryn's leg tremble.

"Oh fuck, baby, you feel so good. I missed you so much," she cooed, tears of joy in her eyes.

Neno kissed away her tears. "I missed you, too baby. But I'm here now and I'll never leave you again."

Lauryn's pussy was sloppy wet as Neno long dicked it, lifting one leg and turning her on her side. He sat up and banged the pussy until Lauryn squealed, "Fuck this pussy from the back!"

Neno turned her over and Lauryn put her pretty brown round in the air. Neno guided himself inside, beating the pussy walls until Lauryn thought she would faint.

"Goddamn this dick is so good! Beat this pussy, baby!" Lauryn urged, feeling her self ready to explode.

Neno spread her ass cheeks and pushed in deeper.

"Make this pussy cum for daddy," he growled.

"Okay, daddy!"

"Cum all over this dick!"

"I ammmm!" she squealed and she did, with Neno cumming right behind her.

"Welcome home, daddy," she snickered, out of breath.

And for the first time, Neno felt like he was home.

Chapter 18

Simair wanted to spend some time with Trinity before making his way down to the club. They met in a schoolyard on Cumberland Street, a couple blocks from the club. When he walked up, he could see the red Charger parked on the pavement. Trinity was sitting on the steps with her gun on her lap. It kind of took him by surprise at first glance, but when she smiled at him, he forgot all about the gun. He knew it wasn't for him anyway. She was just one who stayed on point wherever she was at. When she stood, she passed Simair the gun, having no place to put it. Then she wrapped her arms around his neck.

"Hey beautiful," Simair greeted her in a sexy, low tone. He took in her blue miniskirt, tank top, and Jimmy Choo heels. She looked amazing.

"Hey handsome," she replied, looking into his eyes before pressing her berry flavored glossed lips against his.

The chemistry between the two was electrifying. They slowly took their time getting acquainted with each other beyond the physical. They both wanted to enjoy the raw energy that was present every time they saw each other. Trinity had never been physically attracted to another person the way she was with Simair.

"I'ma be leaving soon," Trinity said, breaking the silence. She smoothed down the crown of her hair and gently tugged on her ponytail.

"Leaving? Where are you going?" he asked with a sad look, tucking the gun in his back pocket.

"I gotta go home soon," she whined.

Her words were like a knockout punch to Simair, who felt like they were making progress. Now his feelings were starting to get involved; he didn't want her to leave.

"So what about us?" he asked, looking Trinity in her eyes.

"I didn't think that far ahead, Simair. I'm a little confused about it myself."

Trinity wanted so bad to tell Simair about Missy wanting to kill Lauryn, but she just couldn't bring herself to betray Missy like that for a man she'd just met a couple weeks ago. This is where all the confusion came from, and before she did anything to hurt either one of them, she'd rather not be around for the drama. She knew for sure that it was about to go down in a big way, and Missy wasn't going to hold back.

"Well look, I got to work tonight. How about tomorrow I pick you up and we can go somewhere and figure dis out? I don't want to lose you," he said, wrapping his arms around her. "Can we do that? Can I come get you in the morning so we can talk?"

"Yeah, we can do that." She gave him another kiss and swallowed the lump in her throat. Trinity wanted to cry at the sadness it brought to Simair's face after hearing she was leaving him.

"Now you're not gonna leave, are you?" he joked, picking her up off the steps and wrapping her legs around his waist.

"No. I'm not leaving. In fact, I was thinking about chillin' wit' you at the club tonight." She laughed, leaning in to kiss him again.

"That sounds like a good idea. I want you to meet somebody anyway."

Simair looked around at the empty schoolyard, and then out to the street where no one was paying them any attention. With her still in his arms, he walked her around to the back of the school, hiked up the miniskirt around her waist, and pressed her up against the building. No panties made her sweet goods easily accessible. She was with it too, encouraging him to keep going by kissing him passionately while her arms remained wrapped around his neck. Before she knew it, Simair had unzipped his pants, pulled out his dick, and shoved it into her soft, wet kitty. He began digging into her guts, and at the same time softly biting down on her bottom lip. She gasped, taking it all in as she rubbed her hands up and down his back.

******

Sayyon snickered at Bianca, who was trying her best to give him some head. She couldn't suck dick worth shit, and she found it hard trying to fit all of it in her mouth and suck it at the same time. It really wasn't the seven inches Sayyon was packing, but rather the girth. She couldn't get her mouth open wide enough without her jaws starting to hurt. Sayyon's width was the main reason she wasn't any good at it. Bianca was his wifey, and he never wanted to look at her like the many whores he had sucking his dick. She was pure and innocent. He was the only person she had ever had sex with, and that's how he was going to keep it. Bianca, on the other hand, wanted to learn how to please Sayyon so he wouldn't have to get it from anybody else.

"Yo, you suck at this, and I don't mean in the literal sense," he joked, lying flat out on the bed.

She smacked him on the side of his leg. "Practice makes perfect," she said, waving his dick back and forth across her lips.

"Yeah. Well, we gotta get you something else to practice on." He grabbed the sides of her head and pulled her up on top of him.

She climbed on top of him and sat right on his dick. He didn't even have to guide it in, and the warm, tight feel of her pussy reminded him why he didn't need to get head from her. His dick fit inside of her like a glove. She rocked her hips back and forth, grabbing his hand and placing it on her breast. Her pussy got wetter and wetter the more she swayed. He was starting to feel and hear gushing, so much that he could feel the tingling sensation of a nut about to erupt. This was all within two minutes of her performing. He couldn't hold it back and didn't want to for that matter. He held onto her hips and guided his dick deeper, squirting his cum up into her stomach. She could feel the warm cream deep inside her. She just looked down at him and smiled.

"I bet I don't need any practice to do that," she teased, holding up two fingers to let him know how many minutes it took.

Before he could comment, his cell phone began vibrating on the nightstand. He wasn't going to answer it, nor was Bianca going to let him answer it, but Sayyon saw that it was Boonchie. The timing was crazy. He had just been thinking about him and trying to figure out how he was going to help him get back on his feet. But Boonchie was on some other shit. He had a way of getting back on his feet, but Sayyon wasn't going to like it.

"Yo. What's good, bro?" he answered, looking up at Bianca who was still rocking back and forth slowly.

"I need to holla at you," Boonchie said in an aggressive manner. "You at da crib?"

"I need to holla at you too, but I need a couple days until I make dis move and I got you. Just fall back for a second."

"Are you at da crib?"

Sayyon thought fast with his answer. "Naw. I ain't at the crib. Why? What's up?"

The phone went dead. Sayyon looked at the phone to see if he had hung up. He did, which sent a red flag up in Sayyon's head immediately. He pushed Bianca to the side of the bed, got up, put his pants on and grabbed the Glock .40 out of his dresser. Boonchie just didn't sound right, and if he thought for one second that Sayyon wasn't on point, he had another think coming.

"What's wrong, babe?" Bianca asked, getting up and putting some clothes on too.

"Nothing. Just stay in here," he instructed, leaving out of the room and closing the door behind him.

He crept down the steps with caution, aiming the gun in front of him. When he got to the bottom of the steps, he went straight for the couch, reaching under it and grabbing yet another Glock .40. After securing the whole downstairs, he walked over to the window, pulling the curtain aside slightly. He couldn't see anything outside on the clear street, but he wasn't about to be content with that. For the rest of the night he sat on the love seat right in front of the window, two Glocks in hand.

******

Missy sat at the blackjack table, tapping her card for a hit. She wasted no time putting her plan in motion, and so far she was doing well. It just was no way in hell she was going to move over two hundred grand in counterfeit money in one night. It would take longer than she expected, especially since Trinity wasn't nowhere to be found to help her out. Nevertheless, she sat there playing a couple good hands before cashing in.

Even though Missy thought that she was being slick cashing out after a few hands, the pit boss caught on fast. Once she took the opportunity to cash in another round, Tony called Tristian over to the table and informed him of what he believed was going on. Tristian couldn't believe it. He overlooked the pretty face, fat ass, and big titties.

"Miss, can I have a word wit' you?" Tristian asked, walking up behind Missy while she was cashing in.

Missy turned around with a sweet and innocent look on her face. She looked even prettier up close, and for a second, he had to remember the reason he was there.

"Is there a problem?" she asked with the sexiest smile.

Tristian grabbed her by the arm and pulled her to the back of the casino.

"I hope you didn't think you could launder money in this casino and go undetected," Tristian said, looking down at his watch.

"I wouldn't call it laundering." She smiled. "Like the many people you got in ya casino, I'm a drug dealer. I change my small bills for larger bills, so I won't have to walk around with large stacks of money."

"You know that's illegal," he said with a smirk.

"This whole club is illegal." She also smirked. "Let's put it this way. I'm changing bills, and y'all are the only ones making money because I usually lose before cashing out."

"Well, let me see ya bills," he asked, wanting to make sure they weren't counterfeit.

Without hesitation, she reached into her pocket and grabbed a stack of twenties. Tristian took one of the bills and held it up to the light, confirming the barcode running through the bill. In his eyes, she wasn't passing off fake money. But little did he know, all he needed was some soda to find out the truth. As crazy as it seemed though, she was making a lot of sense about the casino profiting. But then again, she really didn't have to make any sense with Tristian now looking down at her 36D cup breasts. Missy caught onto his lustful thoughts and decided to make the best out of the situation. But not for nothing. Tristian was a handsome man. The possibility of him getting a shot of pussy was up in the air.

"Look. How about I give you my number? You call me at a later date, and we can go over compensating you for keeping this between me and you," she said in a seductive voice.

Looking at her body and her pretty ass face, Tristian thought about fucking her into tomorrow. His dick even hardened at the notion. "Yeah. I think we can work something out," he said, whipping his cell phone out to take her number.

Chapter 19

Two weeks later . . .

An all white, 2012 Maserati DTS pulled up in front of the club, catching everybody's attention. Lauryn looked at the car and had a weird feeling of who might be inside. When Sayyon got out of the car, all she could do was smile, seeing her baby brother stuntin' as hard as he was. Dressed in a cream Prada linen short set, Gucci belt, and a pair of tan Gucci loafers, Sayyon was fresh and looked like money. Around his neck was a rose gold chain with ice in it and an iced-out 'S' piece hanging from it..

"Ya ass goin' to jail," Lauryn joked, walking down the steps.

She only heard about what Sayyon was doing in the hood, but this was the first time she'd seen him in a couple weeks. Everything she heard looked like it was true from where she stood. Simair just shook his head, knowing that his lil bro wasn't his lil bro anymore. Sayyon was all grown up now, and instead of just getting his feet wet in the game, he dove in headfirst.

The hood was treating Sayyon with love. He had stepped his game way up in the past couple weeks, upping his cocaine stock as well as expanding his operation. He took over Rutledge Street, another block in North Philly known for getting a lot of money. That street alone was moving over 600 bundles a day, which equated to about $60,000 a day without breaking a sweat. Hancock and Cambria was also moving an impressive 300 bundles a day with ease, which was another $30,000 a day. All this, and it still didn't include the weight he was selling in other parts of the city. Base was loving him, and he was loving Base.

"So what brings you through here, baby boy?" Lauryn asked, looking at the rims on the car.

"I got some business to take care of, so I thought I'd stop by to say what's up."

"Yeah. Well, you need to start coming around more often. I barely see you anymore. And I got to introduce you to my husband," Lauryn shot back with a smile.

"Ya husband? Who da hell wifed you?" He laughed.

"You know I'm still with Neno," she said.

Sayyon remembered Lauryn mentioning his name before, but he never got a chance to meet him. He wasn't pressed to meet him either. He was at a different stage in his life and had a lot going on and really didn't have time to worry about Lauryn's love life. As long as a nigga never put his hands on her, Sayyon didn't concern himself.

"Oh yeah, try to make ya'self available so we can go out to the cemetery to see daddy," Simair added.

"Yeah. Well, we can do that this weekend sometime. Put this number in y'all phone," he said, whipping out his cell.

After giving them the number and saying his goodbyes, Sayyon jumped into his car and pulled off. He really didn't have time to chill too much, because he was en route to meet up with Base to re-up again. A half a million in his trunk wasn't a good look if the police decided to roll up and start searching.

Once Sayyon got to Main Street, he pulled right into the storage company. This had become the regular transaction place ever since he started buying his own work. Two cars sat by storage lot 31, and another car was sitting by lot 40. Base was sitting in his car waiting as usual, but for some reason, he didn't get out right away. Surveying the scene, Sayyon could see one of Base's guards standing off to the side with a crazed look on his face.

Sayyon stepped out of the car, and instead of popping the trunk and grabbing the money, he walked over to make sure everything was all right first. As he made his way to Base's car, he nodded at the guard as he walked by. The guard didn't nod back. Looking at Base sitting in the driver's side of his car, he could tell that something was wrong by the expression on his face. Glancing a little harder, Sayyon could see the barrel of a chrome gun pointed at the back of Base's head. Seeing that, Sayyon turned around, but as he did so, Boonchie came from behind the storage lot aiming a gun directly into his face.

"I like the car and see you lookin' good," Boonchie said, holding the gun firmly.

"Damn, Boonch. Dis what you on?" Sayyon asked, looking him in his eyes.

This was the first time Sayyon had seen Boonchie since that day in the hospital. He didn't even see him in traffic, because every time Sayyon tried to come through the block and pick him up, Boonchie was never there. Ever since the kidnapping, Boonchie held Sayyon responsible, knowing that he had something to do with it. That day, he lost everything, even his loyalty.

"Yeah, man. My uncle just came home and we gotta get back," Boonchie teased, waving the gun at Base's car. "It ain't nothing personal, but I told you, you wasn't ready for the street. All dis shit right here is a part of the game." He smiled.

Base's door opened. He, along with the gunman got out of the car. Neno stood behind Base, cracking him in the back of the head with the butt of the gun, and dropping him to the ground. Base's guard saw an opportunity to run for his gun in the car, but that in itself was a bad idea. Boonchie shot him in his back before he could get the door open. Base turned and tried to grab Neno's gun. He too ended up taking a bullet to the side of his head, knocking him right back to the ground. Sayyon froze. It was going down right before his eyes, and he just knew that he was about to be next.

Neno ran over and popped open Sayyon's trunk, grabbing the black duffle bag from it. They had already taken close to thirty bricks of raw out of Base's car, along with some money, so Sayyon was pretty much the final piece to the robbery. Neno walked back over and stood next to Boonchie, raising his gun and pointing it at Sayyon's head.

"Damn, you gone kill me too?" Sayyon asked Boonchie with a hurtful look on his face. "You supposed to be my man."

"You want me to hit him?" Neno asked, walking up and putting his gun to the side of Sayyon's head.

Looking at his best friend looking back at him, Boonchie couldn't be the one to pull the trigger and take his life. Nor could he stand by and watch somebody else do it either. They'd been through too much together, and Sayyon wasn't even supposed to be there. The robbery was an in and out situation, and it was unfortunate that he pulled up in the middle of it.

"Naw, I'm not gonna kill you, my nigga. But if you try to get at me, I won't be so merciful next time," Boonchie said, lowering his gun.

Boonchie and Neno jumped into their car, and the driver, which was Boonchie's baby's mom, peeled out of the lot.

Sayyon finally exhaled, scared as shit at the thought that he was about to be murdered. He just watched as they drove past him. Just like Boonchie told him and had always told him, it was all a part of the game. One thing was for sure. Sayyon disregarded Boonchie's threat. At this point, getting back at him was the only thing on his mind. He was going to kill not only Boonchie but his uncle too. "Dis shit is a part of the game, too," Sayyon mumbled, walking past Base and getting into his car.

******

Missy walked up and got into Tristian's car looking sexy as ever. The first thing she noticed was a gun sticking out from underneath his lap. It didn't bother her though, because she too had a gun. This was the meeting they were supposed to have before Missy went back into the casino to change more bills, and Tristian swore he was about to get some pussy. Missy could see it all in his eyes. But this wasn't just a meeting for the changing bills incident. Missy wanted to get a better understanding about Lauryn, and if she in fact, was the one behind her brother's death. Up to this point, she still didn't have the slightest idea what Lauryn looked like.

"Now, how much is this going to cost me?" Missy asked, determining how she was going to get his hand away from the gun.

"I was thinking maybe we can start off by having dinner."

"Yeah, then what?" she asked, reaching over and placing her hand on his chest.

"Then maybe go back to my place." He watched as Missy's hand made its way down to his dick.

"Then what?" She unbuckled his pants and reached in to grab a handful of his dick.

"Then you can finish what you're starting," he said, certain he was about to get some head.

Missy rubbed his dick until it got rock hard. She looked him in his eyes as she stroked his shaft up and down. It wasn't as big as she thought it was going to be, and if she had decided to give him some pussy, she would have been disappointed. The more and more she jerked his dick up and down, the hornier Tristian got. Unfortunately, he still had his hand too close to his gun, but Missy was about to change that. She leaned over into the driver seat and kissed the tip of his dick. She could see that it made him move his hand slightly, so she went even further and took his dick into her mouth. He sucked in a lung full of air, feeling Missy's warm, wet mouth around his dick. He took his hand away from the gun and placed it on top of her head, pushing himself deeper into her throat. It felt good to him, but it frustrated Missy, especially since she could taste his pre-cum.

She got what she wanted, seeing his gun sitting under his thigh unattended. In one motion, she reached over and grabbed the gun, but before she could pull back off his dick, Tristian shot off a nut right in her mouth. She damn near threw up, spitting it out onto his leg. Tristian didn't even know that she had the gun. That is, until he opened his eyes and looked right into its barrel.

"We're going to play a game," Missy said, wiping away cum from the side of her mouth. "I ask you a question and you tell me the right answer. If you lie to me I'ma squeeze the trigger. Do you understand?" She took the safety off the gun.

He thought about trying to take the gun from her, but the look in her eyes told him not to try it. Tristian just nodded in agreement, tucking his dick back into his pants.

"Do you know my brother Mark? He was killed a few weeks ago," she asked.

"Yeah. I know him. He used to fight his dog at the club."

"Did Lauryn kill my brother? And before you answer this question you might want to think about it." She pointed the gun closer to his head. "I don't want to kill you. I just want the person who shot my brother."

Tristian had to think about it for a second. This was the ultimate betrayal, and he knew that Lauryn was the one behind it. He looked down the barrel of the gun and then up at Missy. He didn't want to get shot at point blank range like this, and he wasn't about to die for something that he didn't do. It was all about self-preservation.

"Yeah, she did it. Her and her brother Simair," he told Missy, trying his best to make it through this.

She was surprised that he would give Lauryn up so fast, but she was glad that he did. It wasn't enough for her to let him go just like that, but she did have something else in mind.

"I can't believe you came in my mouth," she said, scraping her tongue with her upper teeth.

"I'm sorry," he pleaded.

"Shut da fuck up!" she snapped. "Now, we're gonna play a little game. If you win, I leave out of this car. If you lose . . . well, you know what it is."

Missy started pumping her fist, and for a second he didn't know if she was serious. "Paper, Rock, Scissors?" he asked as if it were a joke.

Missy played paper first. Tristian didn't play anything. "This is only the best out of three," she warned as she started pumping her fist again.

Tristian pumped his fist without wasting any more time. He played rock, but Missy played paper again, squeezing the trigger before Tristian could look up. The bullet knocked a chunk of his head off, leaving brain fragments all over the window and steering wheel. Gun smoke filled the inside of the car, and before she got out, she took in a deep breath of it, exhaling as she stepped outside.

GUN SMOKE

******

Base woke up to the sound of sirens in the far distance. His head was pounding, and he found it hard to see from the blood in his eyes. He struggled to get to his feet, but the police sirens motivated him to stumble to the driver side door to open his car. Clearing the blood from his eyes, he looked around for his exit route while holding the side of his head. He looked at Big Baby, his guard, lying face down on the ground before he got into the car. Calmly, he pulled out of the lot and down Main Street.

******

Bianca could hear Sayyon's car coming to a screeching halt in the driveway and ran straight for the front door. He came storming through it like a madman. He didn't say one word as he went straight to the basement. Bianca knew that the only thing he wanted from the basement was guns. He had a shit load of them in all shapes and sizes.

Sayyon flicked the light on, opening a closet door where all of his firepower was kept. The first thing he grabbed was an AR-15 with an extra magazine, placing it on the table next to the washing machine. Bianca finally made her way down the steps and could see what he was doing.

"Yon, what's goin' on?" she asked in a panic, seeing him strap the bulletproof vest around his waist.

He didn't say a word. Sayyon was on one. He tucked a seventeen shot Beretta under his vest with two extra clips, and then went back into the closet and stood there looking around. Bianca came all the way down the steps and stood at the door of the closet and waited for him to turn around. When he did, she was staring him right in his face. He looked into her sad eyes and could see the tears forming.

"Whatever you about to do, can you please think about it, babe?" she said, knowing her pleas weren't going to go far.

KAYLIN SANTOS

It was nothing she could say or do at this point to convince Sayyon not to leave out of that door with those guns. Seeing the look in his eyes, all she could do was step aside.

Chapter 20

Missy walked into the club and headed straight for the second floor, blowing a kiss at Shannon as she passed by the door. When she got to the second floor, it was kind of crowded, and the blackjack table was packed. She waited at the craps table, throwing a stack of twenties on the table. Right before she was about to place a bet, a spot opened up on the blackjack table. She snatched her chips up and headed back to the blackjack table, squeezing into the seat between Linda and Jess. Linda looked over at her like she was fresh meat. Linda stayed at the table and often used other player's mistakes to her advantage. Jess, on the other hand, was on some other shit. He was only there for one reason and winning wasn't it. Not at the blackjack table anyway. Jess was trying to stay out of jail, and working for Agent Razor was the only way he was going to do that.

Digging into her pocketbook, Missy pulled out another stack of twenties, placing it on the table in front of her. When she glanced up, Lauryn stood right in front of her. They both locked eyes for the first time, holding stares for a moment before Lauryn broke the silence.

"To those who don't know, my name is Lauryn, and I will be your pit boss tonight. And she will be your dealer," she said, pulling Erica over.

Missy couldn't take her eyes off Lauryn. She thought that the urge to kill her would take over, but she was wrong. Something about their encounter felt strange. A feeling that she never experienced before sent chills down Missy's spine. Erica tapped the table in front of Missy to get her attention.

"Miss, are you ready?" Erica said, snapping Missy out of her trance.

"Yeah, yeah," she responded, still watching Lauryn walk over to the pit table.

******

Sayyon switched into a less noticeable car once he left his house. During the drive back into the city, all he could do was think about putting a bullet in Boonchie's head. The worst mistake he could have made was keeping Sayyon alive, because it was an all out war at this point. Boonchie had just taken a half million dollars from him. In the streets, the rule of thumb when taking money in that capacity was that you leave nobody behind to try to come take it back. Boonchie was pretty much expecting that, but what Boonchie didn't expect was Sayyon going as far as he was about to go.

******

Missy was hardly able to concentrate on blackjack, trying to jog her memory, or think of anything that would have drawn the connection she was having to Lauryn. Crazy thoughts raced through her head all at once. It was like a light bulb clicked on in her head when she remembered her from George's house the day of Mark's funeral. It became even more confusing to Missy, especially since Lauryn was the one who killed Mark. Visions of her past started coming to her like a freight train head on.

By the time Missy's mind returned back to earth, she had lost eight grand of the counterfeit money in less than an hour, and she only cashed in about fifteen grand. She wasn't focused at all, but one person who didn't have that problem was Linda. She was on fire and glad Missy sat there taking stupid hits.

******

Simair and Trinity finally walked onto the second floor catching just about everybody's attention. Trinity noticed Missy off the rip and winked to let her know that she was there and ready to play.

Trinity only knew how to play craps, so there was no need for her to be around Missy. They were trying to be as incognito as possible, hoping they didn't draw the same kind of attention Missy did the first time when Tristian caught her.

"Oh. She's back again," the pit boss said, walking up and standing next to Lauryn.

"Who?" Lauryn asked, raising her head from the laptop.

"Oh. Tristian didn't tell you? Old girl, Dynasty was in here a couple days ago changing money," he said, catching Lauryn's undivided attention.

"Counterfeit?" Lauryn asked, raising one eyebrow.

"Naw, she was playing a couple hands, and then cashing out right away. I thought she was laundering money, so I told Tristian. He said he took care of it."

Lauryn looked over at Missy, who gazed right back at her. The vibrating cell phone snapped Lauryn out of her stare down. She glanced down at the screen. It was Dough Boy. She assumed he was calling to see if he could come back to work.

"What's good, bro?" she answered, keeping a watchful eye on Missy.

"Yo, turn the TV on," he yelled, sounding like he was crying.

Missy could feel a little tension in the air.

Lauryn, with cell phone in hand, walked across the room and turned on the TV sitting up against the wall. The news showed Tristian's car as big as day on the screen with detectives standing around it. The whole second floor got quiet. Everybody tuned in to the news to see what was going on. Simair walked over after hearing how quiet it got in the room, and he too tuned in to the tube.

The news anchor reported that a man was found dead with a single gunshot to his head. He didn't say any names, but it seemed like everybody in the room knew who it was. Lauryn's jaw dropped to the floor while staring at the screen. She couldn't believe what she was seeing. Tristian was like family, and that's how Lauryn took it. Simair said nothing and just darted down the steps and out the front door. Out of all the guards, Tristian was probably the closest to Simair.

"Shut it down!" Lauryn said to the pit boss, walking over and closing her laptop. "Shut it down!" she snapped again after seeing that he wasn't moving fast enough.

Trinity looked over at Missy and shrugged, not knowing what was going on. Missy knew exactly what was going on. She was the culprit behind the ruined night.

Linda got up, happily having won a couple grand. She was the first one out the door. Lauryn just went to the back of the casino and took a seat on the stool in front of one of the slot machines. She held back her tears, not wanting to show any signs of weakness to the gamblers.

Trinity walked out of the room, tapping Missy as she walked past. Missy had something else in mind. She was tired of playing games with Lauryn. She just sat there and waited for everybody to clear the room.

"What's going on? Why everybody leaving?" Shannon asked as he came upstairs. When he got to the casino, Missy was still seated at the blackjack table watching Erica clean off the tables. Lauryn was sitting in the back with Tony. Shannon walked right past Missy without a second thought and went straight back to Lauryn to find out what was going on.

"Look, Tony and Shannon, y'all two count the money and secure it for the night. We'll open back up tomorrow," Lauryn instructed. "After y'all secure the money, lock up the club. I got to go and find Simair before he do something stupid," she said, rising to her feet.

"What about her?" Tony said, nodding his head at Missy, who remained seated at the table throwing back a shot of Hennessy.

"I'll take care of her," she replied, walking off and heading to the table.

Lauryn walked over to the table, dismissing Erica and sending her home for the night. She stood behind the table, right in front of Missy and couldn't help but stare at her for a moment, feeling like she knew her from somewhere. Lauryn was about to say something, but Missy started the conversation, twirling the shot glass in her hand.

"When I was young, me and my brother used to play this game. We used to play it all day and night. It was a game my father taught us how to play," Missy said, now looking Lauryn in her eyes. "My brother was the best at it."

The more and more Lauryn looked at Missy, the more familiar Missy started to look to her. Her eyes, her hair, and the sound of her voice put Lauryn in a trance.

"Who is your brother?" Lauryn asked, curious as to why she was talking about him so much.

Missy took in a deep breath, and her adrenaline began to pump through her veins. Complete silence seized the moment. For that split second, Lauryn had an idea of who Missy looked like. She put both hands behind her, gripping the gun that rested on her back, just in case her hunch was right.

"You killed my brother over a fuckin' dog! A fuckin' dog!" Missy said, clenching her teeth together.

Lauryn clutched her gun tighter, looking back at Missy without saying a word. She wasn't going to deny it, because there was no benefit in doing so. Missy sounded sure in what she was saying. The conviction in her voice was convincing enough for Lauryn to do nothing other than draw her weapon. When she did, Missy kicked back off the table. As she was falling backward out of the chair, she grabbed the gun sitting on her lap and fired two rounds at Lauryn, one hitting the table and the other whizzing right by Lauryn's face but grazing her neck.

Lauryn grabbed a hold of her neck and dipped off toward the back of the casino, returning fire at Missy, who took cover behind the second blackjack table. Missy was relentless at trying to kill Lauryn, popping up from behind the table and letting go several more shots at Lauryn while walking toward her. A slot machine was the only thing that stood in the way of Lauryn and the flying bullets. It wasn't until Shannon came from out of the small room in the back, firing his weapon, that Missy took cover again behind the craps table. As he shot at Missy, Tony grabbed Lauryn and pulled her into the room. A trap door that Lauryn had installed when she first opened the club provided her the opportunity to escape the building safely with her money and her life.

Missy popped her clip out, grabbed another from her back pocket, and jammed it into her gun. Shannon fired about eight rounds into the table, but was unable to hit Missy through the thick wood. Missy reached up over top of the table and fired a couple rounds off into the back of the casino at Shannon.

Silence took over. When Missy didn't hear any more shots being fired, she slowly got up from behind the table, aiming her gun toward the back of the club. Gun smoke filled the second floor. Once she got to the back of the casino, she could see the door to the small room. She opened fire into the door and the walls, but didn't hit anything. When she kicked the door open, the small room was empty except a few twenties sitting on the table.

Missy glanced around the room. If she had had enough time, she would have searched the room until she found out how they got out. But time wasn't on her side. She knew the cops would be there any minute, so down the steps and out the front door she went.

* * * * * *

Agent Razor walked up and knocked on Mrs. Lincoln's door. It was a little late at night, but she still managed to answer it. After identifying himself, Mrs. Lincoln let him in. Razor came there for no other reason but to show her the pictures he took outside of the club the other night. He spread the photos out on her dining room table. Mrs. Lincoln couldn't really see without her glasses, so she excused herself and went upstairs to retrieve them. During that time, Agent Razor's cell phone started to ring. When he answered it, Jess was on the other end.

"I got some more pictures, and this time it's of the second floor. You can see the whole casino," Jess said, looking down the street from the pay phone he was on. "Oh, and I thought you might want to know that it was a shootout in the casino tonight. I don't know if anybody got shot, but I do know that one of the security guards got killed earlier tonight." Jess looked down at his cell phone and sent Razor the pictures he took.

Razor didn't say anything. He just hung up the phone and waited for the pictures to come in. During that time, Mrs. Lincoln came back down stairs with her glasses in hand. She stood at the table and started looking through the pictures.

"Take your time," Razor said, standing right next to her.

She really didn't have to take her time. Off the break, she noticed Simair standing in front of the club in one of the pictures. She held the picture up to make sure it was him.

"This is him. This is the guy who came from out of his backyard," Mrs. Lincoln said, passing the photo to Razor.

"Do you notice anybody else?" he asked, moving the pictures around so that she could see Lauryn.

She looked at the many pictures, but she didn't notice anybody else. Agent Razor whipped out his cell phone since Jess had sent the pictures. He looked down at them and couldn't help but smile from ear to ear at the pictures of the blackjack and craps tables and several slot machines lined up against the wall. He was so into the photos, he forgot all about Mrs. Lincoln sitting there still looking through the pictures. He quickly asked Mrs. Lincoln to sign the photo of Simair, and then kindly exited her home. As soon as he got out of the house, he pulled out his phone and called the Assistant United States Attorney, Shawn Goldberg, seeing that he had enough evidence to get the warrants he needed to put Lauryn and her crew in jail. Before he even got into his car, he was sending the prosecutor the pictures Jess took for him.

Chapter 21

Tiffany lay knocked out on the couch when she felt a presence standing over her. For a second, she thought it was Boonchie finally coming in, but when she saw the large gun pointing right at her face, she woke completely up, jumping back on the couch.

Next to her lay Boonchie's one-year-old daughter, asleep with her bottle in her mouth. The man standing in front of her had a bandana tied around his face and his hat cocked low over his eyes. Tiffany couldn't even swallow the spit in her mouth, because her throat was dry from fear.

"Where Boonchie at?" Sayyon asked in a low voice just in case he was in the house. The thought of seeing Tiffany pulling out of the lot with his money plagued his brain, but she wasn't innocent by a long shot. If she could do stick-ups with her baby's father, she was capable of getting whatever comes along with it.

"I don't know. He didn't come home yet," Tiffany said, sliding over closer to her daughter.

"Is that his seed?" Sayyon asked, nodding at the baby.

She hesitated but said, "No."

He knew she was lying. The baby looked just like him. "Call him," Sayyon demanded, taking a seat on the end of the couch.

Tiffany grabbed the cordless phone off the table and began dialing his number. The whole time she did it, she kept her eyes on Sayyon. Boonchie didn't answer the phone right away, but when he did, it was like a relief for Tiffany.

"Somebody here for you," she said, passing Sayyon the phone.

"Got damn, playboy. You got a nice family here."

Boonchie was quiet on the other line, looking into the air, frustrated that he slipped and left his family unattended. Even still, he had to play hard, showing Sayyon that this too was a part of the game.

"I can make more kids, Sayyon," he joked. "But then you gotta worry about what I'm a do to you next."

"Boonchie, bring me my fuckin' money and that work. I know too much about you, and you don't really know shit about me. I will run through ya whole family until I kill everybody you love, my nigga," Sayyon threatened, pointing his gun at the little girl on the couch.

"Nooooooo!" Tiffany screamed out, lying over top of the baby.

Boonchie could hear her pleas, and for a second he had to take his ear away from the phone thinking he was about to hear a shot next. He never thought Sayyon had this in him. As he sat on the other end of the phone, he wished he'd shot him in the head when he had the chance. Boonchie not knowing much about Sayyon was also the heart-wrenching truth. Sayyon didn't even have a lot of family left alive in his life, so Boonchie definitely had more to lose than he did. But still standing on his gangsta ways, he stuck to the code of the streets.

"Fuck you, Sayyon. Catch me in traffic, nigga," Boonchie said, hanging up the phone.

Boonchie looked off onto the highway he was driving down, thinking Sayyon didn't have it in him to kill anybody, let alone a kid. He expected his phone to ring again, which it did within seconds. Only when he answered it this time, his baby's mom screamed and a single gunshot silenced her. His daughter's inconsolable crying sounded off in the background, which almost made him crash his car. After about five seconds of hearing his daughter cry, the phone went dead.

Sayyon couldn't bring himself to the point where he could shoot the little girl as well. He just picked up the cordless phone, wiped it down, and pressed 911 so the operator would hear the baby crying. That was enough to get a cop sent to the address immediately.

Boonchie was on fire, and the only thing that could quench it was death . . . Sayyon's.

******

Missy walked into George's house, which was the same house she partially grew up in. Being in the house brought back so many memories, especially the ones when George found out she was pregnant at the age of fourteen. She could vividly remember him calling her all kinds of whores and sluts before kicking her out onto the streets. After she had the baby and George took custody of her, he told her that he put the baby up for adoption. It was the most heartbreaking moment in Missy's life, something she never forgot about. She hated her father with the deepest hatred a person could have.

The house pretty much looked the same except for a few changes. Missy grabbed a picture of Mark from off the mantel and began thinking about him. She missed him a lot and had wished she could have been there to have his back when he got shot. Just thinking about it was getting Missy a little hot under the collar. She opened the back of the frame and took Mark's picture out, stuffing it into her back pocket, seeing as though it looked like it was the only one of him.

Missy couldn't help but notice the many pictures of a little girl hanging up all around the house. The more Missy looked around, she could see that those pictures of the little girl turned into pictures of a teenager. Thinking that it was one of her nieces, she couldn't believe her eyes when those pictures of the little girl turned into pictures of the woman she'd just finished shooting at. The same women who had killed her brother. Lauryn's high school graduation picture blew Missy's mind. "Who da fuck is dis girl?" Missy mumbled, looking around the house.

She walked over to a box sitting in the living room by the couch that read 'photos'. Opening it up, the first picture she saw was of her older sister, Kisha. It made her take a seat on the couch and start looking through the pictures. She sat there reminiscing about the old days, laughing about some things and crying about others. Her heart dropped when she came across a photo that she was well aware of—her daughter's ultrasound picture. Tears filled her eyes, and all she could think about was her daughter. Under the ultrasound picture were a couple more pictures of her daughter after she was born. She looked at her little girl curiously.

Before she could do any further investigating, she heard a car pull up in front of the house. She quickly threw the pictures back into the box, got up, and pulled the 9-millimeter from her waist. Walking over to the window, she could see Lauryn getting out of the car and heading straight for the house. Missy looked around and found a closet to hide in. She wanted to see what Lauryn wanted inside the house, so maybe Missy could get a better understanding of who she was.

As soon as Lauryn walked into the house, the first thing she did was pull her gun out of her back and hold it down by her side. She carried a black duffle bag with her other hand. She didn't know if anybody was in the house and wasn't taking any chances with all that had been going on. Lauryn walked right past the closet and went straight into the basement, stashing away a large amount of cash in case of an emergency. Missy just sat in the closet and watched through a crack in the door.

When Lauryn made it back up the steps, she was on her way out the door when she looked over at the box of pictures. The ultrasound picture sitting on the table caught her attention. She tried to think if she had left it out or not, but once she got up on it and picked it up, nothing else mattered. She stared at the picture and smiled at herself still in the womb. Missy continued to watch through the door, debating whether to come out of the closet. She decided not to, because Lauryn was without question going to start shooting, something Missy wasn't sure she wanted at that moment. Lauryn just tucked the picture into her back pocket and walked out of the house.

Finally, Missy came out of the closet more confused than when she went in. Again she looked at the pictures around the house. Everything was starting to add up. She ran over to the box and grabbed a few pictures of her daughter when she was born. Then she walked over to the youngest pictures of Lauryn hanging on the wall. She looked at the baby picture and then at Lauryn. Missy did that for a few minutes until it hit her. Her head started spinning, and she damn near passed out when she looked into the eyes of both girls. At that moment, Missy realized that Lauryn wasn't just somebody she was trying to kill. At that very moment, Missy realized that Lauryn was her daughter.

She remembered seeing Lauryn at her father's house. The facial expression she wore the night she saw her at the casino, the same facial expression Missy knew as her own. But most of all, it confirmed that feeling, that nagging feeling she felt but couldn't place when she saw Lauryn. Now she knew what it was. Her heart recognized what her head refused to believe.

******

People on the block sat and watched as the SWAT team and members from the United States Marshals, pulled up to Lauryn's club around five o'clock in the evening. Every SWAT officer was armed with a large assault rifle, and on a three-count, the front door to the club was knocked in. Police swarmed the first floor, grabbing and placing under arrest anybody they came into contact with. Shannon was sitting in the back eating his dinner and getting ready for tonight's events. He looked up from taking a bite of his cheese steak and saw FBI written on Agent Razor's jacket. They took him in custody along with the three-man cleaning crew Lauryn hired. Tiny, another guard, was also taken into custody as he came down from the second floor.

Agent Razor darted up the steps with his gun drawn, yelling for the other cleaner to get down on the ground. Everything was still the same way it was when Jess took the pictures. After the whole building was clear, it was time for him to start taking his evidence.

"Bag and tag everything," he instructed the U.S. Marshals, seeing more than enough evidence for a conviction.

He even had people from the Gaming Commission there to help identify where the tables came from. They took blood samples from the basement along with the puppies in the back room. They took just about everything out of the house. The only thing Razor was mad about was the false information Jess gave him about Lauryn and Simair being inside the club. That was a problem in itself. Now Lauryn would find out the Feds were looking for her and go on the run, a part of the job Agent Razor hated.

******

Trinity and Simair lay in bed all day. Simair was still grieving the loss of Tristian. Trinity had a lot on her mind as well. Missy called her right after the shootout at the casino and gave her the green light to kill Lauryn on sight. She was torn between wanting to be in a full time relationship with Simair, or carrying out the hit for the only woman that took her in when nobody else cared. Trinity enjoyed the feeling of being wanted by a man, touched by a man, held by a man, needed by a man and best of all, being made love to by a man. That was a part of life that Missy couldn't teach her. But when it came down to loyalty, her loyalty to Missy was tremendous. Up until now, she felt like she was betraying Missy for the sole reason of getting as close as she was to the brother of the enemy.

They both lay in bed next to each other, allowing their minds to wander as they listened to soft music playing through the speakers. They were so far off in La La Land, that neither of them could hear what was going on right outside the condo. Local police lined up outside the door, and it only took a swift kick from one of the officers for the door to fly open. Simair barely heard the banging noise over the music, but it was enough for him to open his eyes.

He was considered armed and dangerous, so the cops weren't taking any chances with him. The sound of music playing in the back room alarmed them to the possibility of somebody being in the house. After clearing the rest of the rooms, they strategically lined up near the last room. On the lieutenant's command, they kicked the door in and stormed the room. Simair and Trinity lay in bed snuggled under the covers. Red beams covered the blanket, and all Simair could do was throw his head back onto the pillow in frustration.

Both his and Trinity's gun were sitting on the dresser, but without a second thought, Simair claimed them both so they wouldn't lock her up too. He was led out of the house in nothing but his boxers and a pair of house slippers. Trinity looked on and wished that she could have done something to help, but she couldn't. She watched as they put him into the backseat of the patrol car and drove off.

******

If it wasn't for the fact that Lauryn was driving the new car Neno bought her, a white 2012 Cadillac CTS Coupe with a V6 engine, she might have gone to jail when she passed by the club going down Cumberland Street. She definitely wasn't about to stop and find out what was going on, especially seeing FBI and U.S. Marshals written over a number of jackets. Looking into the rearview mirror at the cop lights flashing, she felt like her run was over. With Neno recently coming up in the game, all Lauryn could do was think about leaving the state and starting over somewhere else.

Seeing her cell phone lighting up in the console, Lauryn hesitated to answer it. Although the number was blocked, she took the call anyway. "Yeah," she answered in a low sad voice, looking off onto the road.

"Ya brother just got locked up," a female voice said into the phone and then hung up.

Automatically, she thought it had to be Sayyon, so she called him first. His cell went straight to voicemail, so she then tried to call Simair. His phone went straight to voicemail too. She didn't know what to think or who it was that was locked up, so she just pulled the car over and called the Roundhouse police station to see if they had either one of them in custody. After arguing with the district for a minute, she found out that neither of them were in custody. What she didn't know was that it wasn't the state that had Simair in custody, but the Feds. Lauryn didn't even think twice about calling them.

She was just about ready to pull off from the parking spot when out of nowhere two black Dodge Durangos pulled up and blocked her in. Two men from each truck jumped out. Lauryn didn't know what was going on, and for a second she thought the suit-clad men were the Feds. Out of instinct, she still reached under her seat to grab her gun, but before she could get it out, four men surrounded her vehicle with large caliber guns pointed right at her. She froze.

Base slowly got out of one of the trucks with a .50 caliber Desert Eagle resting in his hand and his head wrapped up in bandages. He walked up to the window, tapped it with his gun, and told Lauryn to roll it down. Cautiously she did, not taking Base as a threat at this point. If he wanted to kill her he would have done it.

"Where's your brother Sayyon?" he asked through clenched teeth.

"I haven't seen him. Why? What's going on, Base?" she asked, looking up at him in fear.

"I think ya brother and his friend Boonchie set me up. They robbed me and did this to my head," he said out of anger.

Lauryn put her head on the steering wheel out of frustration. She did her best in warning Sayyon about the dangers of getting in the game. This was the kind of shit she was talking about. But it was one thing she knew that her brother wasn't into and that was robbing people. He'd rather hustle for his, so it had to be a good explanation behind the incident. Whatever the explanation was, Base wasn't trying to hear it anyway.

"Look Lauryn, we go way back and I know you can make this right. I'm only doing this as a courtesy considering our friendship. I personally wanted to kill you and ya brothers, but I told myself I would give you a chance to fix it."

"Yeah. Whatever you need, Base," she answered, willing to do anything to keep her life.

"I'm glad you said that. They took thirty bricks of cocaine from me and a little more then two hundred grand. I need a million dollars flat. Plus, I need ya brother to give me the nigga who shot me," Base said, looking off down the street.

"A million, Base?" Lauryn shot back, shocked that the number didn't add up to what was taken from him. She didn't sell drugs, but she was well aware of the prices from when Simair used to sell it.

"Look. It's not a negotiation. Get me what I asked for by tomorrow or you already know where I'm at wit it," he said, nodding for one of his men as he walked back to the car.

Before Lauryn could roll her window up, one of Base's men walked over and cracked Lauryn in the face with the butt of a shotgun, knocking her out. When she came to, the trucks had pulled off, and the side of her face felt like it was broken. She couldn't even move her jaw. Blood started to fill her mouth. She opened the door, leaned over, and just let it run out of her mouth. Base did that just to let her know that he wasn't playing any games at all about that money, and it was effective because Lauryn understood completely.

Chapter 22

Boonchie sat outside of Ms. Gladys's house trying to explain what happened to her daughter Tiffany. There was no way he could tell her the truth about the matter, and he found it hard even trying to lie about it. No matter how he looked at it, Tiffany was under his care and security, and as her man, he failed in being her protector. In fact, it was actually Boonchie that put her in harm's way in the first place.

Ms. Gladys wasn't trying to hear anything Boonchie had to say, and she damn sure wasn't going to let her only granddaughter go. That was all she had left of Tiffany, and she was more afraid that something might happen to the baby if she let her go with Boonchie. Boonchie didn't even put up a fight. He didn't have time to take care of his daughter right now. He had to worry about his own life. Not only that, but he also had to worry about the detectives. The longer he sat around her family, the more questions everybody started to ask. He walked over, kissed his daughter on the head, and left. He had one thing on his mind and that was revenge. The only thing he didn't take into consideration was that Sayyon felt the same way, but was more aggressive with it.

******

Missy sat at the kitchen table at Spoon's house smoking a Dutch filled with hydro, something she hadn't done in years. Everything changed for Missy after finding out that Lauryn was her daughter. She was more confused now than ever.

153

When she was young, and she and her father George went through their conflict, she was under the impression that Lauryn was living a happy life with a nice family somewhere. George had lied to her and kept her away from being a mother to her child. Then he had the nerve to put her out the house at the age of fifteen. For quite some time, Missy had been calling around to foster homes trying to find out where her daughter was living, and the whole time she was still living in the same place where she left her, at home. Missy was happy in a sense that she finally found her baby after all these years, but she was also torn by the fact that Lauryn had killed her only brother. One thing was for sure— Missy no longer had the craving to kill Lauryn. What mother was capable of killing her only seed? But on the flip side, she really didn't know where to start at trying to be a mother to Lauryn this far along in the game.

"Oh shit!" Missy blurted, thinking about her giving Trinity the green light to kill Lauryn on sight.

Missy's motherly intuition to protect her offspring kicked in. She darted upstairs to the bedroom and grabbed the rental car keys from off the nightstand, and then shot out of the door. She hoped it wasn't too late, but she knew that once Trinity agreed to do something, nine times out of ten, it was going to get done.

******

Boonchie pulled into his apartment complex, hoping he could get a little rest before going back out to look for Sayyon. He wasn't worried about anybody running up on him here, because nobody knew about this place, not even Tiffany. As he was getting out of the car, his cell phone rang. He had a gut feeling who the caller was, and he wasn't about to answer it until he looked down at the screen. It wasn't Sayyon like he thought. It was his mother.

"What's up, Mom?" he answered, walking toward the building.

"What you thought I was playin', nigga?" Sayyon asked, standing over Boonchie's mom at gunpoint.

The sound of Sayyon's voice on the other end of the phone almost made him shit his pants. He stopped mid-stride, not even getting his key in the lobby door. The sound of his mother and his aunt in the background crying sent a sharp pain through his chest. The crackling noise near the phone also caught Boonchie's attention.

"Damn, nigga. You at my motha's house?" Boonchie asked in shock. "You know I'ma blow ya fuckin' head off when I catch you," he said, walking back to his car.

"Just like I told you, nigga. Get my bread or I'm a kill everybody you love," Sayyon said calmly into the phone.

"Tell ya son what I got in my hand," Sayyon said, sticking the phone out so he could hear his mom.

"It looks like some type of taser gun. Please, son. Give . . ." she said before the masked man snatched the phone away.

"Yo, I swear, my nigga. I will put fifteen thousand volts of electricity in ya mom, and continue to put a steady flow of it into her until she dies," Sayyon threatened, but was more than serious. "I promise she'll die in the worst way."

Boonchie could hear the crackling of the electricity. He didn't have to think about it at all. It wasn't any amount of money in the world worth his mother's life. He didn't want to admit it, but Sayyon really had him by the balls with this one. His mom was probably the only person in this world that could make Boonchie comply, and he did, willingly.

"Yon, man. Don't do nothing to my mom, my nigga. She ain't got nothing to do wit' me and you. I'll give you ya money, just let me know where you want me to meet you," he said in the most scared, submissive tone Sayyon had ever heard from him.

Sayyon could hear the fear and regret in his voice, and for a second, it made him think about everything he was doing. He looked over at Boonchie's mom and his aunt, and felt a little guilty about having them in the position they were in. Especially since he and Boonchie's mom were somewhat cool. And even though she didn't know Sayyon was the one behind the mask, it still felt wrong. This beef was between him and Boonchie, and the only reason he came this far was because Boonchie wasn't trying to show his face. The benefit of it all was that Sayyon's harsh tactics got Boonchie in order.

"Take the money and the work to the church on 57th and Christian Street in two hours. Drop it off behind the pulpit. Say two Hail Mary's and keep it moving," Sayyon instructed.

"Done. How do I know Mom's is safe?" he asked, looking for assurance.

"Unlike you, nigga, I stand by my word when I give it. But trust and believe that if you play games with the drop, it's not going to be about the money anymore," Sayyon warned before hanging up the phone.

As promised, Sayyon left without laying a finger on Boonchie's mom or his aunt.

******

Lauryn kept the icepack on the side of her face while Neno sat at the table putting the money through the money machine. Stressed out and worried that Sayyon still could not be reached, she had to find him in order to find the man who shot Base. A few times she thought he was already dead or possibly in jail. Neno sat there the whole time biting his bottom lip in anger because his girl was sitting on the bed with a swollen face. She couldn't get into the specifics about why her brother owed the mob a million dollars, and that was because she really didn't know. That also made Neno mad. It was to the point where he was about to say fuck giving up the money and just going straight to war with them. Lauryn wasn't stupid though. She knew the capabilities Base possessed, and knew the best thing for her to do was pay the tab and deal with Sayyon when she saw him. It was either that, or bury her little brother, and possibly even herself.

One of Lauryn's cell phones sounded off on the nightstand. When she looked over, her business phone was going off. She picked it up, but the number was blocked. She thought that it might have been Base calling to see if she was ready with the money, but when she answered it, Simair was on the other line. The federal agent afforded him a phone call hoping he would lead them to Lauryn.

"Bro, where the hell are you?" Lauryn asked through the pain in her mouth.

"The Feds got me," he said and then hung up the phone.

That was all he needed to say. Those words alone meant more than the FBI agent standing next to Simair understood them to be. Lauryn always knew that she was going to have to deal with the Feds one day doing the things she was doing. Ever since the day she started the casino, she had an exit plan for when they came.

She immediately dropped the icepack from her face, got up and walked toward the bathroom, breaking down the cell phone in the process. She took the SIM card out of it, flushed it down the toilet, and then smashed the rest of the phone into little pieces. Neno looked at her like she was crazy and didn't even ask what that was all about.

"Yo, we short about a hundred grand," Neno said once the machine stopped.

Lauryn walked back into the room, grabbing her other phone in an attempt to call Sayyon again. Just like before, there was no answer. If anybody should have been kicking up some money, it should have been him. She really didn't know how much she had in her stash house, but she was sure that it had to be at least six or seven hundred grand. Neno put up two hundred and fifty grand of his money, and if given a little more time, he could have gotten rid of some of the cocaine he came up on and had the rest of the money. The new house he just put a huge down payment on, also took up a lot of his money. But he had to secure another home immediately in case the Feds just took Lauryn.

Lauryn had less than twenty-four hours to come up with the rest of the money, and it seemed like the clock on the wall was moving fast. This was the time when Lauryn regretted leaving two and a half million dollars in her house, only for the Feds to have confiscated it.

Chapter 23

Boonchie parked two blocks away from the church Sayyon suggested. He reached down under his seat and grabbed a 9-millimeter Glock, cocking it back to put a bullet in the chamber. He tucked it into his back pocket when he got out of the car, grabbed the money from out of the backseat, and proceeded down the dark street toward the church. The whole way down the street to the church his heart was racing, thumping like a rabbit's foot, feeling like this drop was going to end in a vicious shootout. He still wondered why Sayyon decided to make the drop in the church at eleven at night.

Boonchie walked up the church steps and tried to open the door. It was locked, so he walked around to the side and found the door open. Boonchie had never been in this church before, so he didn't know where to go. It was dark as hell and smelled like an old abandoned building.

Boonchie pulled the gun from his back pocket as he walked around the building, passing through the gym and up a couple flights of steps. He came out of a door that was right behind the pews. He could see the pulpit, but was cautious just to walk down the aisle.

"Ay, Yon. I'm here, dog. What do you want me to do?" Boonchie asked, hoping Sayyon would answer, so he would reveal himself.

Sayyon didn't respond, but he watched every move Boonchie made. He didn't have any intentions on killing Boonchie right now, especially in a church. But Boonchie definitely was going to get some understanding about what was going on.

Boonchie slowly walked down the aisle toward the pulpit with the duffle bag on his shoulder and his gun in his hand. He had to admit to himself that this was some scary shit. For a moment, he almost wished a gun battle erupted just so it would break the odd silence in the church.

Once up at the pulpit, he placed the bag right next to it, and then walked away, heading back down the way he came. He was more cautious leaving than he was coming.

Sayyon watched from a small window as Boonchie finally exited the building. He quickly came down from the balcony seats with the large AR-15 assault rifle in his hand. After making it through a small maze of doors, which led him to the pulpit, he got to the bag and unzipped it. He could see bricks of cocaine and some money sitting on top of it. It didn't look like the half million they took out of his car, so he sat there and looked through some of the stacks of money.

Boonchie cracked the door open and saw Sayyon kneeling down by the pulpit looking into the bag. He had walked to the corner of the block and then turned around in order to catch Sayyon picking up the money. After coming back into the building, he walked back through the church and found his way back to the door behind the pews. He tried to creep out, but the door made so much noise, it echoed throughout the church, quickly catching Sayyon's attention. Boonchie didn't have any other choice but to come out as fast as he could and try to get the best position. He wasted no time opening fire on Sayyon, who dipped behind the pulpit and slapped the safety off the AR-15. Boonchie fired shot after shot as he slowly walked down the aisle, sending flashes of light throughout the dark church.

GUN SMOKE

Even through the hail of bullets flying his way, Sayyon jumped from behind the pulpit and let a countless amount of bullets go in Boonchie's direction. Boonchie dived in-between some pews, but the bullets kept following him, knocking chunks of wood from the pews onto his head.

Boonchie's gun sent flashes of light through the church, but Sayyon's gun lit the church up like somebody turned on a light.

Silence took over in the church as the gun smoke settled in the air. Both men sat still, trying to figure out where the other one was located. "You thought I was going to let you leave this church with that money," Boonchie yelled out through the silence.

"Fuck you, nigga. Now I'm a kill you," Sayyon said, sending several more bullets into the pews.

"You bitch ass nigga. Dis what I do!" Boonchie shot back, coming from behind the pews sending a couple shots back at Sayyon, forcing him to run and take cover behind the choir booths.

Boonchie walked down the aisle with his gun aimed at the choir booth. As he got close enough, he dipped behind the pulpit, a mere fifteen feet from the choir booths. He took in a deep breath, closed his eyes, and thought about his mother on the phone crying. That was enough to make him jump up from behind the pulpit firing. He walked up to the booths firing back to back so Sayyon wouldn't even have a chance to return fire. The closer he got to the booth, the more bullets Boonchie let go. It was all or nothing at this point. When Boonchie reached the booth, Sayyon was nowhere in sight. The AR-15 sat on the floor in front of a small door unattended.

The sound of crackling behind him caught Boonchie's attention—that same noise he heard on the phone when

Sayyon was in his mom's house. By the time he got a chance to turn around, Sayyon fired fifteen thousand volts into his back sending his body into shock, literally. Boonchie dropped to the ground instantly, and was knocked out cold. He should have known to be careful with all the doors inside the church.

Sayyon calmly walked over to Boonchie's limp body, grabbed him by his ankles, and dragged him through the church and out of the side door.

******

The urge to kill Lauryn, turned into the urge to protect her, even if it was from jail. As Missy drove down the quiet street, she found herself pulling up to her brother's house. She got out of the car and stood in front of his house, looking up and down the street both ways at the addresses on the houses. She pulled the small piece of paper out of her pocket that she got from Spoon earlier that day. He had gotten Mrs. Lincoln's information from KiKi, who had memorized it after seeing it on the detective's notepad when they interviewed her for the second time. Missy didn't have to look much further. Nosy ass Mrs. Lincoln was sitting in her living room staring out the window right at Missy.

Missy walked over to the house as Mrs. Lincoln kept a watchful eye, and when Missy started walking up her steps, Mrs. Lincoln reached for her house phone. She didn't know Missy and wasn't about to take any chances knowing she couldn't identify the female who was suspected of killing Mark.

"What do you want?" Mrs. Lincoln yelled through the window when Missy got on the porch.

"Hi. My name is Tina, and my brother lived next door to you," Missy said in her most innocent voice. "I was wondering if I could have a word with you. Pleeeaaase!" she begged.

The old lady didn't take Missy as being a threat, and even though she was a nosy old lady, she still had somewhat of a heart. She put the phone down and moseyed over to the door, unlatching several locks before getting it open. She cracked the door open slightly, looking up and down the street to make sure Missy was alone. She was. Mrs. Lincoln stepped aside and allowed Missy to come in.

Once inside, Missy took a good look around to make sure Mrs. Lincoln was alone, which she wasn't. Mr. Lincoln heard his front door open and came down stairs to see who it was. It didn't bother Missy any. He could get it too.

"Mrs. Lincoln, the detectives told me that you might have seen who came out of my brother's house the morning he was killed."

"Baby, I'ma tell you just like I told the police. It was a young girl and a man that came out of that house. I already picked the guy out in the picture," she said, walking back over to sit down in her chair.

"Well. What about the girl?" Missy asked, seeing if she said anything about Lauryn.

"I really couldn't see the girl. I didn't tell the detectives this, but if I seen her again, I might be able to identify her too."

That was enough for Missy's ears, hearing that Mrs. Lincoln had the potential to put her baby behind bars forever. She sat there a little while longer engaging in small talk about the dogs and other things Mrs. Lincoln remembered about her brother. The whole time she had plotted and planned a vicious murder in her head.

"Mrs. Lincoln, I want to play a game with you," Missy said, grabbing a chair and pulling it in front of Mrs. Lincoln.

"Oh baby, I'm not playing any games." Mrs. Lincoln laughed, looking back out of the window.

Mr. Lincoln just flagged both of them off and headed back upstairs. Missy, on the other hand, wouldn't take no for an answer. Mrs. Lincoln was going to play whether she wanted to or not. Once Missy started pumping her fist, Mrs. Lincoln withdrew her attention from the window and put it on Missy, who played scissors first. Mrs. Lincoln smiled and put her hand on top of Missy's hand.

"Paper, rock, and scissors. Baby, we used to play that when I was a kid." She laughed.

Her sweetness was making it hard for Missy to go through with putting a bullet in-between her eyes, and that was something Missy never had a problem with since she started killing. Then again, Missy never had to kill a sweet old lady before, and for the first time, Missy stopped playing her game of life or death.

"Okay, Mrs. Lincoln. I'ma be leaving now," Missy said, standing to her feet.

Mrs. Lincoln stood up too, leading Missy to the front door. Although Missy was unable to put a bullet in Mrs. Lincoln's head, that didn't mean she wasn't going to kill her. Lauryn's life depended on it. When it came down to it, Missy's daughter meant more to her than Mrs. Lincoln, even though Missy had just found out about her child.

As Mrs. Lincoln headed to the door, Missy wrapped her arms around her neck in an attempt to strangle Mrs. Lincoln. Although she was a little old, Mrs. Lincoln put up a good struggle, backing Missy up all the way to the couch. She fell back, but kept a strong hold around her neck. Mrs. Lincoln's arms flapped around as she desperately gasped for air. It wasn't long before the flapping arms stopped, and Mrs.

Lincoln was dead. Her eyes were still wide open as her body rolled out of Missy's arms and hit the floor.

Missy got up and was about to leave when she thought about Mr. Lincoln, who had gone upstairs. She knew there was no way in hell she could leave him behind. Grabbing a pillow from off the couch, Missy headed up stairs, calmly and slowly as if she were Jason. Mr. Lincoln was a different story than Mrs. Lincoln, so it was no surprise when Missy pulled her gun from her back pocket. She searched every room on the floor, unable to find him. That is, until she heard the toilet flushing in the bathroom. She swung the door open while he was still sitting on the toilet. She walked in, pressed the gun up against the pillow and squeezed the trigger twice, striking Mr. Lincoln in his chest, killing him almost instantly. The pillow muffled most of the sound, but gun smoke filled the bathroom. Missy turned and left the house not feeling any type of way at all. She really had issues.

******

After Lauryn lay down to try and get some rest for tomorrow, Neno took it to the streets. He had a lot of shit on his mind, but even more shit to get off his chest. He felt some type of way about how the streets were treating his girl, especially the most recent incident. He was still contemplating whether he should kill whoever it was that had Lauryn's face swelled up. Being as though Lauryn refused to tell Neno who it was, it was nothing he could do about it. But what he could do something about was Spoon, who had tried to kill Lauryn over Mark. He was well aware of Spoon, and Spoon was well aware of Neno. Neno didn't know what the future held for him and Lauryn, or what was going to happen tomorrow when Lauryn dropped off the money. But he wasn't about to let Spoon think that he was going to get away with shooting at her without consequence.

Speeding on the highway, Neno made it into the city in a little more than an hour. It took another fifteen minutes to get around Spoon's hood. The first time he drove by Spoon's house, a female was sitting on the steps looking like she was just catching some night air. Neno didn't care who she was, and if she was there by the time he parked his car and made his way to the house, she was just going to become a casualty.

******

Trinity sat outside of Spoon's house waiting for Missy to come back. All night she had been thinking about everything that had transpired thus far, and concluded that she was going to go through with the hit, but she had to get out of the city as soon as it was done. There was no way in the world she could still be with Simair, knowing that she'd killed his sister. Even though it could have been done without him knowing, it still would never sit right with her. Nevertheless, Missy was Trinity's girl. They'd been through a lot together, so that's where her loyalty stood.

While Trinity sat on the steps sipping on a Corona, she noticed a man walking up the block. At first, she thought it might have been Chink coming to see Spoon, but as he got closer she didn't recognize the face. She didn't take him as a threat because niggas always walked up and down this street in the late night, so she didn't pay him too much attention.

Trinity downed her Corona, and then looked down to put the bottle on the step. When she looked up, she looked directly into the barrel of the gun.

"Bitch, act like you know," Neno hissed.

Trinity's survivial instincts kicked in, and she reached out in a flash to knock the gun away. If Neno hadn't been on point she would've succeeded. He evaded the move, then backhanded the shit out of Trinity, drawing blood from her mouth. He grabbed her by the hair and shoved the gun in her face.

"Oh, you a tough bitch, huh?"

"Niggah, you the bitch! You need a gun for a girl," she spat back.

Neno chuckled coldly and snatched her to her feet.

"Make another sound and you gonna find out if I'm bitch or not," Neno seethed, and from the sound of his voice Trinity knew he was dead ass.

She complied and kept silent. She didn't know the reason he was there and didn't want to become the reason either.

Neno shoved her inside and closed the door behind them.

"Where Spoon at?" he whispered, sitting her down on the couch.

The moment he asked that, Spoon came walking out of the kitchen with a Styrofoam platter in his hand. He was looking down at his food, but when he raised his head he was looking down the barrel of Neno's gun. He froze, dropping his food to the floor. Neno still had a handful of Trinity's hair, so she still couldn't go anywhere.

"Is this her?" Neno asked, wondering if Trinity was Mark's sister.

Mark knew exactly who he was referring to and shook his head no. He had no idea how he was going to get out of this predicament, and neither did Trinity. All they both could do was think about getting to their guns. Spoon's gun was upstairs in his room and Trinity's gun was only across the room on the windowsill, which Neno was totally unaware of.

Chapter 24

Boonchie woke up in the backseat of Sayyon's truck. As soon as he moved, he could still feel something sticking out of his lower back. Sayyon kept the charge in him, so that whenever he wanted to, he could send another dose of electricity through Boonchie's body. Sayyon kept one hand on the steering wheel and the other on the trigger of the stun gun.

"Stay down and don't say a muthafuckin' word unless I tell you to, or I'ma fry ya ass again," Sayyon threatened, holding the taser gun up so Boonchie could see it. "You know dis shit ain't have to be like dis," he said, pulling over on a dark street. "We could have been rich by now, my nigga, but you had to go and fuck shit up."

"Nigga, you got me 'napped," Boonchie yelled out in anger, but calmed down once Sayyon raised the gun up again.

"Got you kidnapped?" Sayyon asked with a disgusted look on his face. "You dumb muhfucka. I ain't get you 'napped. What da fuck would I have to do that for? I'm gettin' money, and you wasn't holding me up the least bit, my nigga."

Boonchie felt stupid as he sat back there thinking about it. Sayyon didn't have any reason to take anything from Boonchie. All he was really trying to do was look out for him. Boonchie was too high all the time to realize it, and now it was way too late. Their friendship was out the door, and there was no coming back off it.

"But fuck all dat. Where the fuck is the rest of my money?" Sayyon asked, seeing that the bag looked light when he opened it. "And you better not lie, nigga."

"We split everything up. Everything I got is in the bag." Boonchie looked at Sayyon through the rearview mirror.

"Yeah. Well, I'ma only ask you this one time, my nigga, and one time only." Sayyon gripped the taser gun tighter. "Where the fuck is ya uncle?"

******

Neno tied up Trinity and Spoon in the living room with the phone cord and duct taped both of their mouths. He shot straight upstairs and started searching Spoon's room for money and drugs, something Neno knew Spoon was good for. A worthless murder wasn't his style, and he was in need of some quick cash for the drop tomorrow. It wouldn't hurt shaking down the place and getting some money out of the deal before laying them to rest. Neno flipped mattresses, pulled out dresser drawers, and tapped on floors to see if anything sounded hollow. He knew Spoon had something in the house worth taking, so he just kept looking instead of giving up. Once he got to the closet, it was like he could smell the scent of money. His nose was like a bloodhound's when it came to money, especially when it was a bulk of it in one place. He ripped down jackets, opened up boxes, and he still couldn't find it. Nevertheless, he knew it was there somewhere. Neno finally looked up and could see that the closet had a drop ceiling. He just jumped up, grabbed a hold of the string that was hanging from it, and pulled. This was the first time he'd ever seen money falling out of the sky, as the stacks of money fell on top of his head. Two guns also fell from the ceiling, one in which hit him on the shoulder before it hit the floor.

Downstairs, Trinity lay on the floor knowing for sure that this was going to be her last day on earth. She was more upset in the fashion that she was about to die more than anything. She always pictured herself going out in a blaze of glory, not lying on the floor next to a nobody ass nigga like Spoon, who was still knocked out from the blow he took to his head from Neno. She was just about to give up when Chink walked up the steps. Trinity could hear him messing with his keys at the door, giving her a boost of confidence.

As soon as Chink got the door open, the first thing he noticed was the pair of bodies lying on the floor. He tucked his keys in his pocket and pulled the .45 automatic from his waist. He didn't know who was in the house or how many people were in there. So the first thing he did was take the tape off Trinity's mouth so she could inform him of what was going on. The whole time she was pleading for him to set her free, Chink could hear rumbling going on upstairs.

He quickly took the restraints off Trinity's legs and then her wrists, but before she was able to get up, Neno walked to the landing in an attempt to leave. He noticed Chink standing over Trinity and wasted no time letting off three shots in their direction. Chink returned fire the best way he could, aiming up the steps. His bullets backed Neno up into one of the rooms in the hallway. Trinity grabbed her gun off the windowsill, taking the safety off and firing into the ceiling, hoping one of the bullets would hit Neno.

Neno needed an exit, and he needed one fast. With only one clip to work with, he ran back into the front bedroom with the book bag full of money on his back, letting off a few shots as he passed by the steps. The only way to go was out of the bedroom window, which he did, walking down the whole row of houses. As he was walking down the rooftops, he could still hear shots being fired in the house. Trinity and

Chink were under the impression that he was still in the house, so they just kept firing into the ceiling periodically until they realized he wasn't up there. Trinity backed out of the house, looked up and down the street, and was about to walk back into the house when before her eyes, Neno drove right past her. She raised her gun to fire, but when she pulled the trigger her clip was empty. As Neno turned the corner, Trinity thought about it for a second. She wasn't sure what to do. She just said "fuck it," running over to her car hoping she would be able to catch up to him before he was too far away.

******

It took one good electrical shock to get Boonchie to tell Sayyon where Neno lived. He held out as long as he could, thinking Sayyon was going to have a heart and possibly let him go. Wrong. Not only wasn't he hoping to let him go, but it was a 0% chance that Boonchie was going to live. Sayyon was so sure of it, that as they were driving to Neno's house, he asked Boonchie whether he wanted to have an open or closed casket funeral. Boonchie didn't answer him. The question itself scared the hell out of him. How could one know that he was about to be murdered and still contemplate his funeral arrangements? Boonchie couldn't do it, and the whole ride to Neno's house he had to think about it, which was gut-wrenching.

******

Neno walked into the house and headed straight for the bedroom where Lauryn was asleep. Once there, he made it his business to make enough noise to wake her up. She did, sitting up in bed and clearing her eyes of crust. Neno didn't say a word, but rather threw the book bag full of money onto the bed.

"What's this?" Lauryn asked, pulling the bag to her.

"Start counting it," Neno said, walking into the bathroom.

Lauryn dumped the contents of the bag out on the bed in front of her. Her eyes lit up at the sight of all the money. She just shook her head at the thought of Neno always coming through in the clutch. This was one of the many reasons why she loved him so much.

Stacks on top of stacks of twenties lay on the bed, and from the naked eye, Lauryn had counted at least a hundred grand. She got up and went straight to the money machine, plugging it in and taking a seat at the table.

"Yo, I think Spoon might be dead," he told Lauryn, thinking of how the bullet hit him while he was knocked out on the floor. "It looks like I still gotta deal with one or two more people, but other than that everything should be all right," he said, coming out of the bathroom and diving onto the bed.

Lauryn just smiled, stuffing stacks of money in the machine and watching as the numbers showed up on the front screen. Things were really starting to look up, and more than likely, Base was going to have all of his money. Only one problem remained. Sayyon still wasn't answering his phone. He pretty much had the last part of the puzzle, and without it, Lauryn didn't know how Base was going to react. One thing she did know for sure was that if shit got ugly at the drop-off tomorrow, she wasn't going to be the only one that was getting killed. She had her mind made up that if she had to go it was going to be blasting.

******

Sayyon used his locksmith's key machine to get into the back door of Neno's house. As he made his way through the dark downstairs, he drew his weapon and listened attentively to what was going on upstairs. He could hear the sound of what he thought was a money machine in one of the rooms, and the voice of a female talking low. He didn't care who it was, he was going to kill her too without question. Nobody would leave this house alive with Sayyon behind the gun.

Sayyon slowly climbed the stairs, putting one foot in front of the other with his gun aimed, cocked, and ready to shoot. As he got to the top of the steps, he bypassed every room and proceeded to the room where he could hear the machine. Once he got up to the door, it was game time.

******

Lauryn watched as the money machine stopped, and before she could put another stack of money in it, she felt an awkward silence. Following it, the loud sound of the bedroom door being kicked in scared the bullshit out of her. For a second, she thought it might have been the cops, but when she saw her baby brother coming through the door, she froze. With one strike, he kicked the door in and damn near off the hinges. Sayyon was on top of the bed pointing his gun at Neno within milliseconds. He didn't even notice Lauryn sitting at the table, nor did he acknowledge her. He was on point to her every movement though, and had she done anything stupid, he would have put a bullet in her head. Lauryn was so shocked and confused. She couldn't even clear her throat to say anything.

"Ain't no fun till the rabbit got the gun," Sayyon said, looking down on Neno, who was looking back up at him in shock. "Now, you're gonna give me my fuckin' money, or I'ma blow ya fuckin' head off."

"Sayyon!" Lauryn finally yelled out, catching his attention.

He couldn't believe his ears nor his eyes as he looked over at his big sister sitting in front of the money machine in a nightgown. Neno thought this would be a good opportunity to try to grab his gun from off the nightstand, but Sayyon put a bullet in his knee before he could reach it. He did it without even looking at him or breaking eye contact with Lauryn.

"What da fuck is you doin', Yon?" she snapped, getting up from her chair.

Sayyon was hot, and his adrenaline was pumping through his veins like a madman. "You had something to do with this?" he asked, pointing the gun at Lauryn.

He was zoned out and wasn't thinking right. At this point, everybody was a suspect, and he didn't know who to trust.

"You better get dat damn gun out of my face, Sayyon!" she snapped. "And what da fuck is you talking about? Have something to do with what?" she asked, looking over at Neno.

"Dis nigga robbed me and Base a couple days ago. He took a half million from me and was about to kill me," he said angrily through clenched teeth, and then pointed the gun back at Neno, who was holding his knee.

"Who da fuck is dis, Lauryn?" Neno said through the pain.

"Dis my fuckin' brotha, Neno!" she said, putting her head down in disbelief.

The room got silent. Everybody just looked at each other wondering what the next move was going to be. Neno was up shits creek without a paddle. He was the reason why all this shit went south the way it did. He was the reason why Lauryn had to come out of her pocket and pay this million-dollar tab, and of all things, he was the reason why the side of her face was throbbing. She didn't have to think about whose side she was taking, because family always came first in her eyes. But at the same time, she was trying to figure out a way to save Neno's life. That was going to be hard, considering the look Sayyon had in his eyes, and the fact that Base was expecting to have his head tomorrow.

"Yon, whatever he took from you I'll give it back to you. Just don't shoot him," Lauryn pleaded.

Even though the money played a part in it, it was way past that and beyond repair. Neno was the first person to have ever stuck a gun in his face, and Sayyon was gonna make sure Neno was never gonna get that opportunity again.

"Put the gun down, bro, please," Lauryn begged, hoping to come to some type of resolution.

"Naw sis, I can't do dat," Sayyon said, reaching in his pocket and pulling out his cellphone.

"Yon, please!" she yelled.

"I didn't know who you was, dog," Neno pleaded.

Sayyon wasn't trying to hear none of that. He was zoned out and Lauryn could see it. She knew that once Sayyon had his mind made up about something, there wasn't anything that could change it. Lauryn was about to plead for Neno's life one more time, but when she looked into his cold eyes she realized that it was pointless.

"Base, I got both of these muhfuckas," Sayyon said into the phone, still pointing the gun at Neno.

A moment of silence filled the room before Sayyon hung up the phone. The look in his eyes told Lauryn everything. She couldn't watch Sayyon murder Neno, so she just turned and started cleaning the money off the table. Neno could even tell that the phone call wasn't in his favor, but that didn't stop him from pleading.

"Lauryn, don't let ya brother kill me," he yelled before the .45 bullet exited Sayyon's gun and hit Neno in the center of his forehead.

The bullet knocked his body back onto the bed, and just for special effect Sayyon leaned forward and fired four more shots into his face, chipping pieces of flesh all over the headboard. Lauryn just kept bagging the money up, while shedding a few tears. She wasn't sad because Neno died. She really did love him and hoped she could save him, but this was the game. She had no other choice but to respect the game on both sides.

"Base sends his apologies for your face," Sayyon said, before stepping down off the bed and leaving the room.

Chapter 25

Mr. George sat in his room looking out of the window at the other senior citizens dancing outside. They looked like they were having fun, but George certainly wasn't. He hated the nursing home and everything about it. It was like his freedom had been taken away, and the promise of Lauryn coming to take him out every weekend had disappeared into the wind. Two weekends had passed, and she still hadn't been there to see him. He felt alone and wanted to go back home, but he wasn't aware of the dangers it presented if he was left all alone and unattended.

A light knock at his door caught his attention. It was one of the staff members letting him know that he had a visitor. He waved for the visitor to be admitted into his room, thinking that it was Lauryn finally coming to see him. He looked shocked when in walked Missy. She knew where George was after following Lauryn there after Mark's funeral. She looked as though she was trying to disguise herself behind the large, dark tinted glasses and long, straight, blonde haired wig. She came in and shut the door behind her, pulling up a chair right in front of George.

Missy was at her breaking point when it came to George. It was so much built up inside of her that needed to come out. So many things had happened when she was young, that she wasn't able to stand and say anything.

George smiled, stuck his hand out, and began pumping his fist in an attempt to play the game. Missy just sat there.

She wasn't here to play any games, but rather to get some understanding about the things that transpired when she was a little girl. She couldn't help the tears forming in her eyes at the thought of having the conversation she was about to have. After a moment of looking into her eyes, George knew why she was there.

******

Lauryn and Sayyon pulled into the small warehouse just off I-95 where they were supposed to meet up with Base. When they pulled in, they could see heavily armed guards everywhere. Smack dab in the middle of them all was Base, sitting on the hood of his car.

Sayyon jumped out, and then walked to the back of the car, opening the rear door and grabbing a hold of Neno's left leg and dragging his body out to the ground. He dragged the body all the way over to where Base was sitting, and then ripped the trash bag off Neno's head so Base could see his face. He walked back to the car, popped the trunk, and did the same thing with Boonchie's body. Base looked on like he couldn't believe what Sayyon had just done. Even the guards standing around looked on in amazement. He went hard and that was undisputed by everybody in the building.

Lauryn reached for the duffle bag full of money sitting on the back floor of the car. She got out of the car with her shades covering up as much of her face as they could, passing the bag to Sayyon, who walked over to grab it. She took in the whole scenery, looking around the warehouse before locking eyes with Base.

"You good?" Base asked her, trying to be somewhat sympathetic about her face.

"Yeah, I'm good, Base. Shit comes wit' the game, right?" she answered sarcastically, not really good at all.

They held stares for a moment and for a second, Base felt a little guilty about hitting her. He could see the anger in her eyes when she took the glasses off.

Sayyon broke the silence by tossing the duffle bag at his feet. Base looked at the bag, the bodies, and then at Sayyon. He saw something in Sayyon that was priceless. He possessed qualities that most men had to work hard at obtaining, but Sayyon was born with them, and that was a rare thing to find nowadays, even in the mob.

"That's the million in cash you asked for, and I got most of the work back," Sayyon said, unzipping the bag.

"Did you get your money back?" Base asked with one eyebrow up.

"Naw, but I'm good. I ain't got a problem starting from the bottom," Sayyon shot back.

That's just what Base was talking about. Sayyon was willing to give up everything and start from nothing, and it wasn't even his fault why the situation went the way it did. It was no way he could control jealous friends. Base understood everything Sayyon went through. At some point when he first got started, he went through a similar situation.

"Well. Look, take what you lost and leave me the work," Base said, not wanting Sayyon to be the only one taking the loss.

Sayyon put up a small protest, but Lauryn quickly jumped in and offered to take the money seeing as though she was taking a loss too. Sayyon and Base both chuckled at Lauryn's comment, but Lauryn wasn't doing any laughing, going into the bag and grabbing stacks of money. She gave up a lot of money, and she still had problems with the law that she would eventually have to deal with.

"I want you to give me a call when you get ready. I got a place for you here next to me," Base said, getting down off the car and extending his hand to Sayyon for a shake.

"I'm a chill for a while, Base. I got to see if there's something better out here for me," Sayyon said, accepting his handshake and then returning to the car.

"Trust me, kid. With your talents, there's nothing else better for you out there," he said, standing on top of Boonchie's body. And Lauryn, I promise I'm a make that up to you," he shouted before Lauryn got into the car.

******

"Search warrant!" The United States Marshals yelled, kicking in George's front door.

They cleared room after room, but there was no Lauryn anywhere in sight. The house looked empty, and from the dust everywhere it seemed like nobody had been living there for a minute. Frustrated, Razor stood at the front door, placing both his hands on his head as the marshals exited the house.

This was Lauryn's last known address before she bought her own house. Agent Razor wasn't going to stop until he put Lauryn behind bars, and with the recent deaths of Mr. and Mrs. Lincoln, the search for her only intensified. There was no proof that she was involved with the murders, but it was a hell of a coincidence seeing her brother was locked up for killing Mark. Without Lauryn, Razor really didn't have a case against Simair. He could charge him with a lot of things involving the casino conspiracy, but without the head of the conspiracy, the case would go dead. The murder charge was only a single.

******

Mr. George looked from Missy to the window, not saying a word, but keeping this stupid look on his face. They both sat there in silence, and Missy really didn't know where to start. But it was now or never. She was old enough not to be too scared of him anymore.

"What did I do wrong?" Missy asked, fighting back the tears.

George finally took his attention away from the window when he heard the question. "What are you talking about, Modest?" he asked, calling her by the nickname he gave her when she was young.

Missy couldn't believe that he didn't know what she was referring to. It made her mad and the tears in her eyes dried up. It was crazy because she remembered everything like it was yesterday.

"I guess you're going to sit here and tell me that you don't remember the nights you pulled me out of my room to come sleep with you in the bed."

George just sat there with the stupid look on his face. He didn't have to remember, because it was something that he hadn't forgotten. It was something that stuck with him through all these years.

"You don't remember the things you used to do to me while I was in your bed? And you didn't even care that I cried when it hurt," she said angrily through her teeth. "You made me feel like I was nothing."

"Aww Modest, that was so long ago. What's done is done, sweetheart. I can't go back and change what I did."

"I just want to know why. Why did my own father rape me?" she asked.

George sat there and thought about it. It was like all his Alzheimer's vanished and he knew exactly what was going on.

"Modest . . . I'm so sorry."

"I don't want to hear sorry. I want to hear *why!*" she demanded.

George looked at her with a compassioned filled gaze.

"Do you think it will make it any easier? For either of us?" he questioned, shaking his head. The memories had tormented him for years, which was why he always headed for New York. He needed to tell Missy what he struggled to tell her at that moment.

"How can it be hard on you?" Missy questioned.

"Modest, you're not really my daughter. When me and your mom was together, she cheated on me and had you by the man she ended up leaving me for," he explained with the saddest look in his eyes. "I hated that woman so bad. Sometimes at night, I even wished she were dead. She didn't even have the chance to break the news to your real father before she died. I held that against her, and I took it out on you. Oh God, I was such a fool," he cried. Real tears slid down his face.

To hear this coming from George's mouth was heart-wrenching. All Missy could do was listen to the answers she'd been looking for all these years. He lied about so many things and kept so much away from her. It was like her whole life was a lie, and George was the puppet master.

"You got me pregnant!" Missy wept, unable to hold back the tears. "You took my little girl from me."

"Lauryn isn't my baby," George quickly clarified. "I had a blood test done years ago. Lauryn's dad is . . . you know, the boy from down the street." He was unable to remember his name.

Missy knew exactly who he was talking about. Sadiq, her childhood boyfriend was probably the only person Missy could confide in when she was young. It was puppy love, but that was the only time Missy ever loved. She could remember having sex with Sadiq just so it felt like she gave her virginity away to someone she cared about, instead of having it taken away without her consent by someone she hated. She remembered telling Sadiq that the baby was his, but soon after, she was forced to leave Philly and go stay with a aunt in New York that she didn't even know.

George just sat there with a dumb look on his face. He even tried to grab Missy's hand. She quickly snatched her hand away, glaring at him like he was crazy. He turned and stared out of the window again as if this conversation didn't mean shit to him. His attitude seemed to suggest that this was some old shit, but shit like this didn't get old. It never got old, and it weighed down on women like Missy every day.

Missy thought about the day when she found out she was pregnant and how George blamed her for it. He made her look like the bad person instead of taking responsibility for his own actions. She thought about the day when she had Amira Shardea Henderson, Lauryn's real name, and how George took her away after they came home from the hospital. She thought about the day he kicked her out of the house and made the whole family think she was the bad seed. She used to sneak and stay over Sadiq's house as much as she could, but at that time Sadiq was too young to understand anything, let alone try to raise a baby and take care of Missy. He was still living with his mother himself. It got hard fast, living in the city of Philadelphia, and on those nights Missy couldn't sneak in Sadiq's house, she had to sleep outside in the park. It was her sister Kisha who gave her the telephone number and the address to their Aunt Margaret that lived in New York. That's when Missy had to make the choice to stay in Philly and continue to struggle, or take her chances moving to New York. With no money, hungry, and in a deep state of depression, Missy scrambled up a few dollars and caught the next thing smoking out of Philly, a place she no longer wanted to live in.

This was something Missy had to live with day in and day out, and the bad part about it was that she was too young to understand. Now, after all the pain and suffering, and with all of her questions answered, it was time for retribution.

Missy calmly reached into her pocketbook and pulled out a 9-millimeter Taurus and a silencer, sitting them both on her lap. George continued looking out of the window, unaware of what was going on right in front of him. She calmly screwed the silencer onto the gun like it was routine. At this point, she felt nothing else. Missy was numb.

When George finally turned to say something to Missy, the gun was pointed at him and Missy stared him in his eyes. George looked down at the gun and then back up at Missy and smiled. He didn't think she was capable of pulling the trigger, but he was wrong. She released the first bullet right into his gut. It was a pain his old ass had never felt before. And as he reached for his stomach, Missy sent two more bullets into his head, knocking him out of the chair and killing him instantly. The muffled sound wasn't heard by anybody on George's floor. Missy tucked the gun away and took a whiff of the gun smoke in the air. She left the room, putting the "Do Not Disturb" sign on his doorknob behind her.

******

Lauryn drove down Cumberland Street with Sayyon in the passenger side. She really just wanted to take one last look at the hood before she left. Her time in the city was up. Now it was time to move on to other things. She wasn't broke by a long shot, not even before Base gave up five hundred grand. She still had money in George's house that she had put away for this purpose alone. Being as though it was a body warrant, the Feds never found the money. Her only two worries were her brothers, with Simair being the main one. He faced possibly spending the rest of his life in jail for a murder he didn't commit. That weighed heavily on her too. Even though Simair held his water and didn't tell, she wasn't going to let him go down for it. If necessary, she was going to take her own beef.

Then she had Sayyon, who was thinking about what Base said during their drive back to the city. He was already struggling, trying to figure out what he was going to do now. Bianca broke the news to him that she was pregnant and was keeping the baby. At the same time, the bills were still coming through the door. Lauryn still didn't want the drug life for her brother, but at this point she really didn't know if she could do anything to stop him.

Sitting at the red light on 17th Street, she looked over at her little brother and managed to crack a smile. When Sayyon looked back at her and smiled, the look in Lauryn's eyes was strange. Everything went in slow motion, and it seemed like the red light just froze. Lauryn watched as Trinity side stepped across the intersection, whipped out a large caliber handgun, and cupped it in both hands. By the time Sayyon looked over, the first bullet went crashing through the front windshield.

Trinity had been on Lauryn ever since Neno ran up in Spoon's house. Once she stole the opportunity to follow Neno back to his house, everything else was history. She almost lost Lauryn on I-95 a couple of times, but was able to catch back up with her.

"Get down!" Lauryn yelled, ducking behind the steering wheel and stomping on the gas.

Trinity stepped out of the way of the moving vehicle, but continued firing on the car as it went past her. She sent four bullets to the driver's side of the car, and then four more through the back window as the car drove away. The car didn't get far, because Lauryn crashed into a line of parked cars. Trinity popped the empty clip out and shoved another in, running down the street toward the car. Sayyon's door was jammed, but he could see Trinity running up on the car. He pulled his weapon and fired through the side of the window, forcing Trinity to think twice about getting close. Through the dipping and trying to get behind something, she could see Lauryn slumped over the steering wheel. That wasn't enough for her though. She needed to make sure that Lauryn was dead. She aimed and squeezed the trigger, trying her best to hit her from the awkward position she was in.

Sayyon returned fire again, this time having a little more accuracy, hitting Trinity in her arm. She turned and grabbed her left arm in pain. It was time for her to make her exit before she ended up getting killed. She fired the rest of the bullets in her clip into the car as she ran across the street toward her car.

"Lauryn! Lauryn!" Sayyon yelled, shaking her shoulder. Get up, big sis," he said, climbing over her and opening up her door. "We can't stay here," Sayyon yelled, trying to pull her out of the car.

She wasn't moving, and for a second Sayyon thought that she had got hit by one of the bullets. He checked her body to see if he felt any blood but he didn't. She wasn't shot, but she was knocked out from the airbag smashing her in the face. The police sirens in the distance prompted Sayyon to get his sister to her feet and out of the car. He grabbed the small trash bag full of money from the backseat and put it on Lauryn's lap. The police sirens got his adrenaline flowing.

GUN SMOKE

With little time left to act, he picked her up and carried her down the block, as far away from the car as he could get her. It was right on time too. As soon as he turned the corner, two cop cars came flying down the street, surrounding the car they just got out of.

Sayyon managed to get Lauryn up on the porch of somebody he didn't even know. He watched as the police shot by on their way to the scene. He didn't want to draw any attention by lying Lauryn down, so he held her up in his arms like she was his girlfriend. Sayyon quickly turned around once he heard the locks on the door start clicking. He didn't know whose porch he was on, but fortunately, the person did however, know Lauryn very well. Lauryn looked shocked when she finally opened her eyes to see Ms. Linda standing over her, helping her and Sayyon into the house. Ms. Linda was never on point as much as she was today.

Chapter 26

The nursing home was full to the max with detectives, more specifically, in George Tucker's room. One of the nurses was trying to get him to take his medication when she discovered his body lying on the ground. It scared the living shit out of her to see all the blood he had lost. The forensic unit stood over him snapping photo after photo and collecting all the evidence they could, which was none. The video surveillance only showed a blonde haired woman coming to visit him, but they couldn't get a positive I.D. on her, especially since she signed under a fake name.

"Do you have any relative contact information for him?" the detective asked, wanting to notify somebody in his family that Mr. George was murdered.

"Yes, we have his granddaughter. Her name is . . . Lauryn Brown," the administrator said after pulling the file from out of the cabinet and opening it. "I just don't understand what kind of person would do something like this," she said, walking off and taking a seat in her office.

She didn't understand because she wasn't in Missy's shoes, and had she'd been, the results would have been different. George probably would have just gone to jail dealing with a less aggressive woman. Hell, he might have gotten away scott free considering the statute of limitation law. With Missy, the only law she enforced was by the gun. Not a single day would go by that she wouldn't sleep comfortably knowing what she'd done.

GUN SMOKE

Agent Razor was on the scene of the shooting on Cumberland Street within minutes of the first responding unit. He walked up on the gray Chrysler 300 and counted the many bullet holes in the door and window. The car was a rental, and the renter's form in the glove compartment listed the name Lauryn Brown. Judging by the size of the accident, it was surprising to him that nobody was killed. But if Lauryn was in the car, he felt like she couldn't have gotten far. He slowly walked over to the detectives who were leaning over a female body on the ground. His heart was racing, anticipating that it might have been Lauryn, but when he got up close enough he could tell that it wasn't her.

"Who's the victim?" Razor asked, squatting over the body.

"A bystander. Poor girl can't be no older than nineteen," the detective answered.

Razor was determined now more than ever to catch Lauryn. He wasn't going to leave the neighborhood until he did so, or until she left before he could find her. The only problem he had was getting the cooperation of the people in the neighborhood. It was like they loved her and supported her more than they supported the authorities. The Feds or the local cops would never be able to accomplish anything with this type of attitude.

******

Lauryn woke up on Linda's couch after taking a quick nap. She just couldn't figure out why her brother's girlfriend was shooting at her. Not only was she shooting at her, she was trying to kill her. Lauryn couldn't remember doing anything to her for her to want her dead. Hell, she didn't even know anything about her.

Lauryn just sat up on the couch, licking her bottom lip that was busted during the crash. When she looked into the dining room, Linda had Sayyon at the table playing blackjack. He didn't know shit about cards, but Linda didn't mind giving him lessons, especially taking a few dollars from him in the process. Lauryn's cell phone ringing caught everybody's attention. As she rolled off the couch, she answered it.

"Hello?"

"Good evening, ma'am. May I speak to a Ms. Lauryn Brown?" a deep voice spoke into the phone.

"This is she."

"Hi ma'am, my name is Detective Morton from the Grove County police department. Do you know a man by the name of George Tucker?" the detective asked in a sorrowful voice.

Lauryn almost hung up, but when he mentioned Grove County she paused. That was the same county as the nursing home where George lived. She looked over at Linda and Sayyon, who went back to playing cards, and then walked over to the window.

"Yes, that's my grandfather. Is everything all right?" she asked with caution while peeking out of the window.

"Ma'am, I hate and regret to inform you that your grandfather was shot to death early this morning in his room at the nursing home," the detective said calmly.

Lauryn became silent. It took a second for the detective's words to register in her head. Lauryn's heart dropped to her stomach once she realized what was just said. It hit her hard, so much she had to take a seat on the couch before she passed out. It was one thing to hear that her grandfather had died, but it was a totally different thing to hear that he was murdered, shot to death to be more specific. Her eyes filled with tears, but not one of them dropped. Something inside her told her that Mark's sister had something to do with that. Her sorrow was quickly replaced with fury, and the tears in her eyes dried up.

"Ma'am. Ma'am, are you still there?" the detective asked, not hearing a peep through the phone.

"Yes, I'm still here, detective."

"We're going to need somebody to come down to the Grove County Morgue to identify the body."

Lauryn had to think about it for a second. She knew she had warrants out for her arrest and that the Feds were looking for her. All she needed to do was show up at the morgue and get handcuffed right after seeing the body. It was a chance Lauryn wasn't willing to take. For all she knew, it might have been a set up and George really wasn't dead.

"I will be there shortly," Lauryn said, hanging up the phone.

As soon as she got off the phone with the detective, she turned and called the nursing home to make sure it was true. When she finally got the administrator on the line, it was confirmed. She was hoping that it was a lie, but it wasn't. George was dead.

******

Missy reached for her cell phone in the center console as she drove down back into the city. She answered it quickly. Trinity was calling. This was the first time she had talked to her since the night she gave her the green light to kill Lauryn. It was good she called, because now she was finally able to call the hit off.

"Where da fuck have you been?" Missy answered, looking off onto the road ahead.

"You sound happy to hear from me," Trinity joked. "I guess I ought to tell you a bit of good news."

"And what's that?"

"Lauryn's dead. I just shot her car up in North Philly earlier today," Trinity said, looking at the news in her hotel room. "If you're somewhere by a TV, you should turn the news on."

Missy pulled over and parked after hearing the news. She was too late, and as bad as she was trying to protect her daughter, she ended up being the cause of her death. It was like a knife being shoved into her heart. She wanted the chance to make things right with Lauryn, and to be the one to tell her that she was her mother. Missy wanted Lauryn to know everything that happened when she was young, and that she never gave up trying to find her. She wanted Lauryn to know the truth and she wanted the chance to finally be a mother again.

"Goddamn you!" she spat, as the tears spilled from her eyes, and she didn't know if the words were directed at herself or God.

Missy put her head against the steering wheel as the sobs racked her body. Guilt turned to grief, grief into anguish and anguish became anger.

And the face she pictured was one of her closest friends, now turned unwitting enemy.

"Where are you?" Missy gritted, throwing her car back in drive and pulling out of the parking space.

It may not have been Trinity's fault, but it was her doing. Therefore, she had to pay, and Missy wasn't going to rest until Trinity's body was as cold as she thought Lauryn's was.

Chapter 27

J ust in case it was a setup, Lauryn took Sayyon out to
the morgue so he could identify the body.

"Here, take a look at this," Lauryn remarked,
showing Sayyon a picture of her grandfather.

"Come on, yo. You know I know what George looks
like," he assured her.

"I . . . just wanted you to be sure."

Sayyon could see how distraught his sister was. He leaned
over and kissed her on the cheek.

"Everything's gonna be okay, sis. I love you."

His heartfelt words made her muster a smile.

"I love you, too."

******

"Agent Razor," Razor answered.

"Agent, this is Detective Murphy. I've got a break for
you."

"I definitely need one."

"It's about Lauryn Brown. Her grandfather was just
murdered. If you're looking for her I'd try the morgue."

Razor snatched up his keys, heading for the door.

"What made you call me, Detective?" Razor questioned.

"I ran a check on her name and the federal warrant
popped up."

"Quick thinking."

"Yeah, well, if you want to catch her, you'd better be
even quicker getting here."

Razor shot through Philly traffic expertly. He was a man on a mission. He wanted to bring Lauryn down bad, and he feared this would be the best shot he'd ever get. The thought alone made him shoot through the light as it turned red from yellow and just barely avoid a collision in the intersection.

******

Sayyon slid through the few police standing around, with ease. Since he had no warrants the police weren't looking for him, allowing him to slip under the radar.

He walked into the cold room of the city morgue. The walls were lined with cabinets for the bodies, and the room was awash with a cold bluish light. Waiting for him was a detective and a morgue technician. Sayyon approached them.

"I've come to identify the body of George Tucker. He was a resident in the nursing home in County Grove," he announced.

"And you are?" the detective asked, eyeing him coldly.

"The next of kin," Sayyon replied, returning the cold gaze.

The technician nodded, and then walked over to a cabinet. Sayyon and the detective followed. The technician opened the cabinet to reveal George's dead body. Sayyon took one look at the multiple bullet wounds and was glad Lauryn didn't have to see him like that.

"Yeah, that's him," Sayyon told them.

The detective looked at Sayyon, who showed no signs of emotion as he looked down at the body. He looked more amazed at seeing the body than anything. His reaction sent the detective's radar up.

"So, what is your relationship to the deceased?"

"He's my grandfather," Sayyon lied, seeing where this was going. He turned on his heels, leaving the detective with the gnawing feeling that he should go after him.

Sayyon walked out of the morgue, taking his time walking the two blocks to where the car was parked because he knew Lauryn would take the news badly. As he approached the car, another one turned the corner.

Agent Razor's.

******

Razor pulled over and parked, keeping his eyes peeled, but he was looking for the wrong thing. He was looking for a woman, not a man. So when he saw Sayyon, he glanced right over him.

******

Lauryn knew as soon as she saw Sayyon's face that it was official. The pain hit her all at once, exploding out her face in the form of tears. Sayyon just grabbed the top of her head, put it on his shoulder, and held her tightly.

"I'm here, Big Sis."

"I-I know. It's just—hard," she sobbed.

He knew it was the wrong time to tell her about where and how many times he had been shot, but he knew that eventually he would have to tell her. Somebody was going to answer for this, and whoever it was, the cops better find them before Lauryn did.

******

The text saved her.

As Sayyon pulled out, he was heading straight for Agent Razor. There was no way he could've not seen Lauryn. But he didn't, and it was all because his phone rang with a text. The moment he looked down was the moment Sayyon and Lauryn drove by. She was right beside him, so close, all he had to do was reach out his arm and he would've touched her.

That was probably the closest he would ever come to catching her, and he had let her slip through his grasp, and he would never know.

******

Missy pulled into the Holiday Inn out by the airport where Trinity had checked in. She still had on the disguise she wore in the nursing home and was about to take it off until she thought about it. She really didn't know what she was going to do to Trinity, if she was going to do anything at all. After all, it was Missy's call to kill Lauryn. It wasn't Trinity's fault that she carried out the hit. She was only doing what she was told.

Missy made her way up the stairs to the third floor, the whole time weighing everything in her mind. She even stopped on the second floor to take some extra time out to contemplate. Trinity wasn't just anybody on the streets that Missy didn't care about. She'd been looking out for Trinity for years now. Their relationship was similar to a mother-daughter relationship, but in reality she wasn't her daughter. Lauryn was her daughter, and it was Trinity who ultimately pulled the trigger and took her life.

She fought with herself the whole way up stairs. Once Missy got to the room, Trinity didn't make things any better, holding a bottle of Ciroc in the air as she answered the door. She was under the impression that it was going to be a small celebration behind killing the woman who killed Missy's brother. Trinity also had something else she wanted to celebrate too, but the look on Missy's face when she walked into the room told the tale. There wasn't going to be any celebrating tonight.

"What's wrong, Mama?" Trinity asked, seeing the stressful look on Missy's face as she closed the door behind her.

GUN SMOKE

"Nothing, T," Missy replied, taking a seat on the bed and looking into the TV screen.

It was ironic that as she was looking at the TV, the news was coming back on. Even crazier was the Cumberland Street shooting was the top story of the day. The news anchor came onto the screen and explained how an unidentified woman was killed in the shooting. They showed pictures of Lauryn's car crashed and shot up pretty bad. Missy could hardly look at it, seeing that this was how her baby had died.

"That's my work," Trinity proudly said, walking over and taking a seat right next to Missy on the bed. "I got grazed on my arm though." She showed Missy her small bandage-covered wound.

She explained how she found Lauryn and how long it took her to wait for the right moment to strike. She explained how Lauryn crashed into the parked cars, and how she ran down on the car and shot her before she eventually got shot herself.

Trinity didn't even understand that she was only adding fuel to the fire. The more she talked, the more Missy felt justified doing what she wanted to do. It got to the point where Missy didn't even hear anything Trinity was saying, going off into her own land. Missy couldn't help but think about Lauryn. It hurt, and sitting there listening to Trinity brought about a crucial decision.

When Trinity got up to use the bathroom, Missy reached into her pocketbook, grabbed the gun with the silencer still screwed on it, and tucked it in her back waist. Once Trinity got done in the bathroom, she came out to see Missy standing in front of the TV.

"Thanks, T. I love you, baby girl," Missy said, extending her arms out for a hug.

Trinity walked right into her arms, happy that Missy appreciated what she had done. Missy stood there and held Trinity for a moment, kissing her on the forehead and grabbing a handful of the back of Trinity's head. Trinity was so caught up in the moment, she didn't even notice Missy pulling the gun from her back. It wasn't until Trinity pulled back from the embrace that she felt something pressed against her stomach. She looked down at the gun then back up at Missy with a confused look on her face. She wasn't even able to say anything before Missy squeezed the trigger, injecting a hot ball of lead into Trinity's gut. She squeezed the trigger again, sending another one into her. Missy grabbed a hold of her before she could fall to the floor, slowly guiding her body to the ground.

Trinity yelled out through her teeth in pain, feeling like her insides were on fire. Missy couldn't hold back the tears that filled her eyes, looking down at her close friend, who was looking back up at her with a scared look in her eyes.

"You always told me to keep my enemies close and to watch out for my friends," Trinity said, holding her stomach.

"I know. I know. I'm sorry, Mama," Missy responded, placing her hand on top of Trinity's.

"Did I do something wrong?"

"No, no baby. You did good," Missy cried, watching Trinity die right in front of her.

"You messed up my surprise," Trinity joked, finding it in her to crack a smile.

"What surprise, baby girl?"

One of Trinity's lungs began to fill with blood. Within seconds, Trinity started to cough up a little bit of it. She looked at Missy as though she was about to go into shock. She was determined to let Missy know what she had done before she died. The more Trinity thought about it, she began to cry.

"We was going to have a baby," Trinity said, sticking a dagger right through Missy's heart. Her body tensed up and the tears lined her cheeks. "I was going to name her Nahja Maria Rodriguez," Trinity softly spoke as she started to fade in and out of consciousness.

Missy looked down at Trinity's stomach and could see little dark chunks of blood all over her hand. She had no idea that Trinity was pregnant and wished Trinity had told her this before time. She would have never killed Trinity knowing that. Missy just sat there and cried her eyes out as she watched Trinity fade away. Regret set in immediately, but it was too late. By the time she looked back up at Trinity, she had passed away. Missy just reached up with her bloody hand and closed Trinity's eyes before wrapping her up in her arms. Not only did she take the life of her friend, but she also took the life of her baby, and that was something that Missy was going to always struggle living with.

Chapter 28

I t seemed like most funerals happened on a day when it was raining, and George's funeral was no different. Not many people were there. George didn't have much family still living, and if they were alive, they really didn't care much about him enough to come out to his viewing. It was kind of sad, but expected, considering George wasn't as great of a father as he should have been. But to Lauryn, George was like her hero growing up. He took care of her when nobody else was there. That was her grandpop.

As the small crowd stood outside in the rain, admitting George into the ground, Lauryn sat watching through a pair of binoculars from a far distance away. She knew the Feds were going to be there, so she wasn't taking any chances. She didn't drink, but today she was sipping on something light, just to get her through the rest of the day. She couldn't help but think about Missy and how she was the reason for this sad day. Lauryn was going to do everything in her power to find and kill Missy. She wasn't going to leave the city until her goal was met.

As Lauryn looked through the binoculars, she could see an unmarked car sitting near the entrance of the cemetery. Once Razor got out of the car with a pair of binoculars of his own, Lauryn knew he was the Feds. He was working in his typical fashion. Lauryn got low behind a tree, hoping he wouldn't see her watching him. But she was too far in the back of the cemetery for Razor to even think about looking for her.

GUNSMOKE

******

Missy sat and peered through a pair of binoculars, watching to see who showed up at George's funeral. As she took a good look around the cemetery, she couldn't believe her eyes.

She's alive! Missy's mind screamed.

She spotted Lauryn crouched behind a tree all the way on the other side of the cemetery. Her heart dropped and so did the binoculars.

"Oh fuck! What have I done?" Missy seethed, thinking about Trinity.

Her mind raced back to the moment when she had shot Trinity, and each gunshot made her wince.

She had killed her best friend, more like a daughter, simply because she thought she had killed Lauryn. Missy was sick to her stomach. She rolled over on her back and looked into the rainy sky, clenching her teeth in anger.

******

A cemetery worker startled the shit out of Lauryn as he walked up from her blind side. She drew her weapon on instinct, startling him right back. He threw his hands in the air, passed Lauryn a piece of paper he was told to deliver to her. It was obvious Lauryn and Agent Razor weren't the only ones looking at the funeral through binoculars.

"Who gave you this?" Lauryn asked the worker who stood there with his hands still in the air.

He just pointed across the way. Lauryn looked through her binoculars. She could see a woman walking away and leaving out of a hole in a fence on the other side of the cemetery. She knew it was Missy, and if she wasn't so far away, she would have run her down and got busy right then and there.

Lauryn dismissed the man, but not before passing him a few bills and telling him not to tell anybody that she was up there. Lauryn couldn't believe that Missy was at George's funeral, hiding in another section of the cemetery like she was crazy. *She's got a set of balls on her*, Lauryn thought, unfolding the piece of paper that was given to her. She looked at the note and couldn't believe what it said.

Lauryn, you don't know me, but there's a lot about me that you do need to know. Meet me at the casino tomorrow night at 8:00, and I will explain everything to you. Just keep in mind that everything isn't what it seems.

Lauryn read the letter one more time before balling it up and stuffing it into her pocket. Just those few lines had Lauryn's brain going into overdrive. She wondered what she was talking about when she said, "Everything isn't what it seems." Lauryn's thought pattern came to a halt after coming to the conclusion that it wasn't nothing else to think about. It was nothing Missy could say or do to fix what she'd messed up. The only good thing about the note was that Lauryn was finally going to get her chance at retribution. Lauryn didn't have no rap at this point. She was about to let her gun do the talking.

******

The sun had just gone down as Lauryn drove through the streets of North Philadelphia, parking right around the corner from the club. She had on black Air Max's, blue jeans, a black hoody, a black book bag, and a fitted hat cocked low. The bulletproof vest under the hoodie felt a little discomforting, but Lauryn quickly adapted to it by the time she made it to Cumberland Street.

She stood on the corner of the block watching the traffic coming through there, only to make sure that no cops were lurking around. Instead of going through the front door,

Lauryn went around back, using the dogfighter's entrance to get in. As soon as she unlocked the door, she reached in her back waist and pulled the Glock .40 caliber out. She aimed it in front of her as she walked through the door. She looked around the basement and secured it before taking the book bag off her back and placing it on the floor. Cautiously, she unzipped it, went inside and grabbed the silencer, quickly screwing it onto the .40 cal. She pulled a second .40 cal out and did the same, screwing yet another silencer on the gun, but stuffing that one under her vest. She wanted to keep this confrontation deadly but as quiet as possible. Before leaving the bag behind, she stuffed several extra clips into her back pockets, and then readjusted her vest.

Lauryn used the same escape route to make her way through the house, and once she hit the first floor, it was total silence. The whole house was dark except the streetlights that flashed through the windows. For a second Lauryn thought that she might have been in there by herself. That is until she heard the floor creak on the second floor. Then out of nowhere a voice spoke.

"George wasn't who you thought he was," Missy said from somewhere in the house. "He was a monster and he had to die."

Lauryn sat still for a second trying to figure out where the voice was coming from. This was like some shit out of a horror movie, but Lauryn played along, inching her way through the club. The closer she got to the door that led upstairs to the casino, the stronger the voice got. Lauryn doubled back through the first floor and used the escape route to climb to the second floor.

"I know that you came here to kill me, Lauryn, but I can't let you do that. It's something you need to know first."

Missy clutched the seventeen shot Glock 9-millimeter in her hand.

Up the back route Lauryn crept, climbing up to the small room in the back of the casino. She could still hear Missy talking, but really wasn't paying any attention to what she was saying. Before she cracked the door open, she took the other Glock from under her vest, and kissed it on the slide. The voice was at its strongest, so Lauryn knew that Missy had to be right on the other side of the door.

"Lauryn, George was a rapist," Missy said, looking down the front steps.

Lauryn heard those words loud and clear, and that was enough to ignite the fuse. The back door swung open and Lauryn came out firing, sending multiple shots to the front of the casino, forcing Missy to drop to the ground and crawl behind the partition. The sound of the bullets hitting the wall was actually louder than the gun itself being discharged. Lauryn released ten shots, five from each gun at rapid speed, blasting holes through the sheetrock right above Missy's head.

Daughter or no daughter, Missy reached around the partition and squeezed the trigger, sending a few quiet thunderbolts back toward Lauryn. Lauryn's counter strike was almost immediate as she threw ten more shots back at Missy, forcing her to come from behind the partition and run for the steps. Lauryn darted right behind her, but when she got to the top of the steps, Missy was waiting for her at the bottom, firing three more shots at her. One of the bullets hit Lauryn smack dab in the middle of her chest, knocking her backward a little bit, causing her to stumble to the ground. The bullet was caught by the vest, but the impact was like taking a direct hit to the solarplex. The bullet took the air right out of Lauryn.

Missy thought about running back up the steps after seeing Lauryn was hit, but that thought went away fast when Lauryn blindly fired another round down the steps in order to give herself a few extra seconds to get her bearings. Missy dipped off and pressed her back against the wall right beside the steps. Lauryn did the same, sitting up against the wall at the top of the steps. Although Missy couldn't see her, she felt Lauryn's presence close by and knew that she would be able to hear her when she spoke.

"Your real name is Amira Shardea Henderson!" Missy yelled up the steps. "You weighed eight pounds, two ounces when I gave birth to you in Children's Hospital." Missy paused briefly. "And you're right. I did kill George. He was the one who raped me when I was a little girl. I got pregnant with you shortly after."

What Missy was saying sounded crazy and sick. Her words only made Lauryn angrier. The things she was saying about her grandfather . . . Lauryn listened as she took off her vest and climbed back to her feet. Slowly, she walked to the back of the casino toward the escape route. She walked ever so lightly in her Air Max's. Missy couldn't even hear her footsteps pacing around up stairs.

What Missy was saying didn't make any sense at all to Lauryn. She couldn't even begin to consider the notion that Missy could have been her mother, and even worst that George may have been her father. In any event, Lauryn listened to Missy as she slid down the back way.

Missy was trying her best to explain everything to Lauryn, but in her heart she felt like none of it was getting through to her. She really didn't want to kill her only child, but she was in a situation where she didn't have any other choice. Lauryn was relentless and wasn't going to stop until she killed Missy. Once Lauryn had her mind set on doing something, it was going to get done, or she would die trying. Missy knew this because Lauryn was only the product of her mother.

"Amira, if you're listening, please don't make me do this," Missy pleaded. "If you give me a chance I can prove everything I'm saying."

Instead of stopping at the first floor, Lauryn went all the way to the basement, reloading both guns before heading for the front steps that led to the dance floor where Missy was hiding. As she slid up the steps to the door, Lauryn peeped through the key hole. She could only see the side of Missy's body leaning up against the wall, but knew that this was the best chance she had. She put one gun in her front pocket and then turned the doorknob slowly.

At first, Missy wasn't even aware of Lauryn's position. She thought she was still at the top of the steps, but when she felt a draft of cool air coming from her right side, she saw Lauryn coming from out of the basement, guns a blazing as she darted across the room. The small wall Missy hid behind took bullet after bullet, knocking chips of wood into her face. It wasn't big enough to cover her whole body, so she too came from behind the steps firing back at Lauryn. She ran and took cover behind the wall in the middle of the room. Lauryn also ducked behind the same wall, which separated the dance floor from the kitchen. They both squatted with their backs up against the wall, clutching their firearms.

"So this is how it gotta be? You're gonna kill ya own motha?" Missy said, breaking the silence.

"My motha died when I was ten!" Lauryn shot back. "Now come from behind that wall, so I can put a bullet in ya fuckin' head."

"Let me ask you this, Lauryn. Did you ever go to your mother's funeral when she died? Did you ever see her get buried?"

Lauryn sat up against the wall thinking about what Missy just said. She never did go to a funeral when her mother died, and that was one of many things she didn't understand when she started to get older. Even though George told her that her mom was cremated, it still bothered her.

"I know this might be hard for you, but did George ever ask you to put makeup on and call it a dress up day? Did he ever ask you to sleep in his bed after the make-up party?"

Lauryn thought about what Missy was saying. She went back as far as she could, trying to remember. She did remember having a couple of make-up parties, but it wasn't the way Missy was making it out to be. The few times George did come get her out of her bed to come sleep with him seemed innocent. Lauryn couldn't remember him doing anything to her sexually. She didn't remember any sexual abuse at the hands of George at all, but she did feel kind of funny sleeping in the bed with her grandfather at the age of eleven.

"Did you ever feel something wasn't right about it, but you didn't say anything because you were scared?" Missy continued.

Lauryn popped her clips out to see how many shots she had left. At the same time, she couldn't stop thinking about her childhood and if anything seemed out of pocket when it came to George. The more she thought about it, something that Lauryn remembered but had forgotten about until now surfaced out of nowhere.

"Did you ever feel his dick against you when you were asleep in his bed?" Missy asked, bringing herself to tears.

Hearing those words, Lauryn snapped out of anger. She turned, fell to her back and opened fire on the wall in front of her. Missy stood, turned, and then fired into the wall too. Lauryn let everything go, yelling at the top of her lungs as blue flames spit out of her gun. Bullets from Missy's gun pierced the sheet-rocked wall and whizzed right by her head, but Lauryn continued to fire.

At the same time, one of Lauryn's bullets came crashing through the wall, hitting Missy once in her thigh and another in her side. She took the bullets but didn't fall, and kept firing back into the wall until her clip was empty. Missy too let everything go in her clip. After a brief moment of silence, only the sound of clips falling to the ground in order to reload could be heard.

Lauryn struggled getting the clip out of her back pocket and into the gun. By the time she did, Missy was standing over her with her gun pointed right at her head.

"Drop the guns!" Missy demanded, pressing the gun up against Lauryn's head.

She hesitated for a moment, but dropped the guns that Missy swifly kicked across the room. Lauryn looked up at Missy and knew that she was about to die. She braced for the impact, closing her eyes, clenching her teeth, and balling her fist. Missy lifted her hand from her stomach to see how much damage the bullet did. She looked at Lauryn and had thoughts of splattering her brains all over the wall, but Missy was still instinctively a mother and just couldn't do it. She lowered the gun, walked over to the corner of the room, and grabbed a little black bag. The whole while she kept Lauryn at gunpoint. When she got back over to Lauryn, she fell to her knees in pain, placing the gun down by her side. Lauryn looked confused, not expecting to still be alive at this point. Missy reached in the bag and pulled out a few pieces of paper and passed it to Lauryn. Lauryn hesitated, but took the papers, holding one of them up to the light. It was a birth certificate with a set of footprints on it. The name Amira Shardea Henderson was written across the top. Behind it was also a social security card and a few pictures of Missy holding Lauryn in the hospital after she was born. The baby in the picture looked just like Lauryn's baby picture that she took from George's house. Only this time the baby was being held by her mother. The next photo was a family picture of Sadiq, Lauryn's father, sitting in a chair holding Lauryn, with Missy standing up behind them.

Lauryn sat up on her knees and looked into the eyes of her biological mother for the first time that she could remember. She could feel the connection, just the way she did the first time she met her in the casino. Tears filled both of their eyes as Lauryn leaned in for her mother's embrace. Missy wrapped her arms around Lauryn's shoulders, pulling her head into her chest.

"Hey, baby," Missy cried, kissing Lauryn on the head.

"Hey, Mom," Lauryn responded, wiping tears from her face as she laid her head on Missy's chest.

Suddenly, Lauryn could feel Missy getting heavier, and before she knew it, her mother had collapsed. Missy was losing too much blood from the bullet wound to her side. Lauryn quickly took her hoodie off, wrapped it around her mother's waist tightly in an attempt to stop the bleeding. Missy looked up at Lauryn for what she believed to be for the last time, and smiled.

"I love you, Amira," Missy managed to get out before her eyes started to roll to the back of her head.

"You better not die on me!" Lauryn cried. "Please don't die on me now, Mom," she continued to yell as she picked her up and carried her out the front door.

Chapter 29

Three months later . . .

After dropping her mother off at the hospital, Lauryn wasted no time getting the hell out of the city, considering the fact that she saw her face big as day on the ten o'clock news while she was sitting in the hospital. Atlanta wasn't that far of a place to relocate, but it was going to do for now. It was kind of slow compared to the fast city life of Philadelphia, but it had a lot of potential. Lauryn could see a vision the minute she stepped into the city.

Lauryn sat on the passenger side of the car with a blindfold on, not knowing where she was going. Sayyon said he had a surprise for Lauryn for her birthday and didn't want her to see it until she got there. The ride was taking a while, and being blindfolded was starting to irritate Lauryn. It seemed like once she was at her breaking point, the car stopped. She couldn't help but start smiling at the thought of what Sayyon had in store for her. She was pulled out of the car and led inside a building where it was a little chilly. It was quiet and smelled like an old warehouse, but when Lauryn took the blindfold off, she was standing smack dab in the middle of what looked to have been a bar. It was huge, complete with a thirty-foot bar, an upper deck level, and an extra large dance floor.

"What is this, Sayyon?" she asked, looking around the place.

"This is your new place." He smiled, leaning up against the bar. "It cost me a few hundred grand, but I think I could afford it," he said with a devious grin. "Come on. Let me show you the rest of the place." He led Lauryn to the back of the bar and down a set of steps.

When they reached the basement, Sayyon hit a light switch that lit up the whole floor. Lauryn couldn't believe it, looking at a mini casino right before her eyes. It had three blackjack tables, three craps tables, two Russian roulette tables, and about fifteen slot machines lined up against the wall. It was very spacious and damn near looked like a real casino floor.

"Oh shit! Thank you, lil' bro," Lauryn said, giving him a big hug.

"Hold up, sis. I'm not done yet," he said, walking over to the bar and pushing a little button to speak into the intercom. "Come on in," he said into the speakers.

From a small door hidden on the side of the casino, out walked Missy, Simair, and Bianca. They all appeared to be in picture perfect health. She hadn't seen anybody but Sayyon since the day she left Missy at the hospital. To see everybody in one place at the same time was the best birthday gift Lauryn could ask for—that, along with the mini casino Sayyon put together for her. Lauryn just sat there speechless, and as she walked into the arms of her family, she felt the love all around. She looked around the room and could see the potential of having the strongest family to ever hit Atlanta yet.

READING GROUP
DISCUSSION QUESTIONS

1. What was the significance of the title? Did it resonate with you as a reader?

2. How did you feel about the dog-fighting scene that opened the book?

3. Was Lauryn justified for shooting Mark over her dog? Why or why not? Did it make you believe the author is a dog lover?

4. What was the most gripping scene for you?

5. Who was your favorite character? Least favorite character?

6. The moment Sayyon noticed Boonchie falling off. Should he have ended their partnership earlier based on that fact? Why or why not?

7. Was there any quote or dialogue in particular that stood out for you?

8. Would you have been as faithful to Missy as Trinity was? Explain?

9. Should Missy have forgiven Mr. George? Or were his past acts undeserving of forgiveness? Explain your answer.

10. Did your opinion of the book change from beginning to end? How?

11. What did you think of the relationship between Simair and Trinity? Would it have lasted? Explain.

12. Was Lauryn justified in killing Neno? Why or why not?

13. If you could give any of the characters a 'beat down', who would it be and why?

14. Was the end satisfying?

15.   Would you be interested in reading a sequel? Explain.

W·CLARK
PUBLISHING

Nude Awakening II
Still Naked

A Novel by

Victor L. Martin

<u>Theme Song:</u>
Kendrick Lamar
"Don't Kill My Vibe"

CHAPTER
One
Ain't No Future Right for Me

January 20, 2012

Friday 3:10 PM – Miami, Florida

T his some real live bullshit!" Trevon muttered behind the wheel of his newly painted gem green 2010 Jaguar XJL. "I knew they was gonna find that bitch ass homo thug not guilty!"

Seated next to Trevon, LaToria aka Kandi settled back into the black leather seat with her arms crossed. "Swagga ain't worth the stress," she muttered, tight-lipped with a frown.

"I know," Trevon replied, staring at the courthouse up the busy street. "I just can't get over what he did to you . . . or what he did to us!" he added, punching a tight fist into his right palm.

LaToria closed her eyes for a moment. "We got to move on from this."

"It ain't easy," Trevon said, slumping back into the seat.

1

She turned her head, looking into his eyes. "You got too much to lose. Ain't trying to raise this baby by myself, Trevon."

"I wouldn't dare risk my freedom for that bitch ass coward!"

"Well, we both need to move past this and focus on us and our baby." She laid a hand on his knee. "Ain't trying to lose you."

Trevon looked at her belly. In the month of June, she would bare his firstborn, and it was a moment that he was looking forward to. "What we gonna do about this film?" he asked.

LaToria shrugged. "I don't think anyone will really care about Swagga fucking that tranny. With our luck, he'll find some way to make it blow up in our faces. Besides, with Chyna dead, I don't see nobody giving a damn, and that's just how I feel."

Those words fell hard on Trevon. In truth, he had too much at stake to focus on any type of revenge toward Swagga. Money had proven stronger than truth, and it had set Swagga free. Not guilty was the verdict of the kidnapping charge against Swagga. His high-powered team of attorneys argued heavily that no one could firmly prove that Swagga had actually kidnapped LaToria and taken her aboard his yacht. They turned their focus on Swagga's former bodyguard, Yaffa.

Trevon had to accept the reality and remember the chance he was being given behind killing Yaffa in that warehouse. Even still, he was having trouble letting shit ride behind his beef with LaToria's ex. As she had just mentioned, they were still in possession of the two video clips of Swagga and Chyna. LaToria was leaning toward the idea of moving up to Atlanta with Trevon, leaving

Swagga and the stress and past behind. Exposing Swagga's homo tastes would only bring drama back into their lives.

"I wanna go home," LaToria said, gazing out the tinted window at a black couple sitting at a bus stop. Both were in their own world, chatting away on a cell phone.

"You ain't going to Amatory with me?"

"Nah." She shook her head. "I'm tired, and plus my feet are hurting."

"Told you not to wear them heels so—"

"Look," she interrupted. "He's coming out!"

Trevon sat up the moment Swagga made his exit from the building. A roar of cheers went up from the mass of spectators that awaited Swagga's appearance. Trevon's tight jaws flexed at the sight of Swagga standing on the top step with his skinny arms raised joyously in the air. He was surrounded by his legal team and ten-deep entourage. The bright sun danced off the pricey diamonds that filled Swagga's mouth.

Trevon took it all in with silence. He could see Swagga taking a pose on the steps in front of a group of photographers while the crowd worked itself into a frenzy.

LaToria turned her head, forcing herself to let go of her anger. All that mattered in her life was the baby and loving Trevon.

Trevon pulled the XJL from the curb with the tinted windows lowered two inches. He didn't speak until he reached the first stoplight on Biscayne Boulevard.

"You thought about what we spoke on last night?"

LaToria sighed. "Don't make a big deal of it, Trevon. You signed the contract, and it's business, so I'm okay with it."

Trevon glanced at her, trying to understand how she was so at ease with him going forward with his contract with Amatory Erotic Films. He was willing to opt out of the contract for the strength of his relationship with her. LaToria assured him that she wouldn't trip. She told him she saw no wrong with him doing five more films.

"You gonna be okay?" he asked, reaching for her hand.

She nodded. "I just need to lie down, that's all."

When the light turned green, he drove the sleek sedan past a Burger King on his left. Looking ahead, he switched lanes while pushing his thoughts to the bright side of his life. His biggest joy was his freedom. He knew he had a rare chance to live the life he did by doing adult porn. How many ex-cons could boast of the life he had? Damn few! Trevon refused to risk his freedom again. Killing Yaffa last year was done in a rushed rage. But even now he held no regret, nor a touch of remorse. He had killed for a woman he was deeply in love with.

Reaching Coconut Grove, he parked his Jag behind LaToria's brand new soft-top diamond black Aston Martin DBS. After walking her inside, he glanced out into the backyard to check on his bullmastiff, Rex. He lay on his side in the shade, asleep. Kissing LaToria on the cheek and giving her plump ass a squeeze, he turned to head for the door.

"Trevon." LaToria stood in the living room with an odd, troubled look.

"Yeah, what's up?" He turned, standing in the door.

She just stood there, unable to speak what was on her mind.

"Baby, you sure you're okay with me—"

"I'm fine," she said in a rush. "Just bring me something to eat on your way back home."

NUDE AWAKENING II: STILL NAKED

"Pizza or chicken?" he asked, grinning.

She forced a smile. "Both," she replied. "I'm eating for two, remember." Trevon paused at the door with an inkling that Latoya was lying through her teeth. Though she wore a high voltage smile, her eyes told him differently. Not wanting to stress her out, he kept his view to himself.

***

Twenty minutes later, Trevon was seated in front of Janelle's office desk inhaling her light peach-scented body spray.

"I heard the news about Swagga," she said after Trevon was comfortable in the chair.

"Yeah, LaToria didn't take it too well."

"I'm not surprised about that."

Trevon removed his smartphone from his pocket to make sure the ringer was off. "Sorry 'bout that," he said, keeping his eyes above her breasts. The purple satin blouse clung tight against her perky twins. She was dressed professionally in a pantsuit that did little to cover her natural sex appeal. He managed to avoid any lustful looks at her.

"Well," she said, leaning back in her chair. "Are you ready to discuss your future here with Amatory?"

"It's why I'm here."

"So, what have you decided?"

Trevon wanted to make the right choice. "I'll finish out my contract and do the rest of the films."

"I assume you and Kandi have discussed this at some length?"

"Yeah, but mainly I was the one stressing it. She said it won't bother her for me to continue to do porn without her."

5

Janelle nodded at the wall to Trevon's left. "Don't take this the wrong way, but Kandi knows how to draw the line between her emotions and business."

Trevon looked at the cover art posters of the DVDs that were produced by Amatory. "She told me that herself. But being honest, I told her I couldn't stand to watch her be with another man. So you know I'm happy about you allowing her to opt out of her contract."

"I already knew that, Trevon. I won't force you to do the films. I'm really happy for you and Kandi, but at the same time, I don't want to leave money on the table. By you doing the last five films, I promise you that you'll be set financially."

"I don't doubt that," he said, thinking of the money still being made off the fast-selling DVD he made with LaToria. With each DVD sold, he earned $1.80. Trevon's future looked straight if his next five DVDs could sell like the first. Last week, Janelle had sent him and LaToria an e-mail to inform them of the success of their DVD ranking number one in sales. In less than four months, the DVD had reached a number of 375,000 copies sold! He was looking forward to his first royalty check.

"Have you read the latest reviews on your DVD?" she asked.

"Nah, been too busy with going to the gym and running errands for LaToria. Umm, did someone post something bad?"

"Nope. Far from it." She smiled. "Each day your female fan base is growing. Anyway, a fan posted a review saying how she loved the film and how much she envied Kandi. She gave the DVD five stars and asked if there would be more DVDs with you in it."

NUDE AWAKENING II: STILL NAKED

Trevon, in all truth, tried to stay grounded and humble. From ex-con to porn star was not an everyday switch. "Umm, I guess we gonna grant her request, huh?"

"Most surely!" Janelle replied, motivated.

Trevon adjusted his thoughts to focus on his actions as just business. He was sure of his love for LaToria. It was an issue he didn't doubt nor question. "When do we start filming?" he asked.

"Later next month." She reached for her laptop. "Here, I want you to look at something."

Trevon found himself briefly dwelling on whom he would be making his next film with. His thoughts were broken when Janelle turned the screen of the laptop in his direction.

"This is Chelsea Kelliebrew. I signed her last month to a four-film deal right before the Christmas holiday, and I'd like her debut film to be with you."

"She looks young." He observed.

"She's only twenty-two, and she's a very nice girl. Being with her will cover your venture into interracial films."

"She a true blonde?"

"Yep. She's five-foot-six and a former swimsuit model. She looks so much like Lindsay Lohan."

He nodded in agreement. "What will the theme of the film be?"

"It's still up in the air right now. But I did inform my screenwriters that I want it to be outdoors. The bedroom scenes are becoming the norm," she explained. "Also, I want you to do an anal scene with her. Are you okay with that?"

Trevon sat up, rubbing a hand down his face. His conscience was tearing at him. Even if it was just *business*, he felt wrong to be casually making plans to fuck another female. He looked at the image of Chelsea modeling a two-piece yellow string bikini. There was no need to deny how sexy she was, even for a white girl. "I'll do it," he finally said, after thinking on it.

Janelle lifted her arched eyebrows. "I'm not getting the vibe that you're *sure* about doing this."

"Uh, have you told her about me yet?"

"A little. By now she has viewed your video with Kandi. Trust me. If you want to be a top-seller, you have to do interracial films. Though it's not my favorite." She shrugged. "It's business and business is money."

"I don't doubt you one bit. It just feels like I'm doing LaToria wrong," he admitted. "I guess I need to stop mixing my work with my private life."

"Just do what's in your heart, Trevon. If you need some time to rethink—"

"Nah, I'm good." He sighed heavily, allowing his shoulders to slump. "I said I'll stick to the contract, and that's what I'm gonna do."

Janelle hoped his actions would match his words. "And I won't doubt that, Trevon."

"So, when will I meet her?" He nodded at the picture of Chelsea.

"Sometime next week. She's moving down from Orlando and should be settled in her new spot soon."

"Ai'ight. So what's the deal with the other films?"

"I'd like to have you doing a different class of subject with each film. With Chelsea, you'll be doing interracial like I said, so the other films will differ."

"How?"

"Well, I'd like you to do a film with a plus-size female and one with an older woman. Also, I think a threesome is a good idea as well. I have a few more ideas, but the interracial film with Chelsea is a must do. For the record, interracial films are always top sellers."

Trevon turned his attention back to the picture of Chelsea.

"She looks even better in person," Janelle commented. "And FYI, she has never been in front of a camera, so this time you'll be the teacher."

"Hell, I'm still learning the ropes myself." Trevon leaned back in the chair. "Oh! What does FYI mean?"

Janelle smirked. It had slipped her mind that Trevon was still a newbie when it came to today's terms. "It means for your information."

"I'll have to remember that." He grinned.

Janelle turned the laptop off and then fingered a loose tress of raven black hair over her shoulder. "So how's life really treating you?"

Trevon shifted in the chair. "This drama with Swagga gettin' off free has me pissed! I know I did my dirt as well behind what went down in that warehouse. But still, Swagga tried to burn LaToria alive, and I just have to stand by and watch this nigga ease off the hook."

"Would you feel better if he went to prison?"

Trevon balled up his hands. "I can't ever wish prison on anyone. Not after doing all that time I did."

"You can't let this problem get the best of you. Like you just pointed out, you yourself were lucky with not being charged with killing Swagga's bodyguard. Just move on, Trevon. Let it go. Focus on your future with LaToria and the baby."

"I swear I'm trying," he said, being honest with himself.

"Try harder. Do it for yourself, Trevon."

He nodded.

After a few exchanged words about the new film, the meeting came to an end. It was official. Trevon would continue his career in the adult film industry with Amatory Erotic Films.

"Is there anything else that's troubling you that you'd like to talk about?" she pressed.

Trevon wasn't sure if he should open up to Janelle. The truth was yes. He had another issue troubling him, but he assumed she would view him differently if he spoke on it. Biting his words, he lied and said that everything was all good.

***

Strolling to the back of Amatory's private parking lot, Trevon continued to dwell on the choice he made. It was only business, he reminded himself. Nearing his Jag, he took a glance at Janelle's Lamborghini Aventador, wondering if he would one day own a high-priced whip as such. Not downing his XJL, he was content with it and the triple chrome Rucci rims 24's it sat on.

Easing behind the steering wheel, he reached for his shades off the dashboard. Times such as now, he was filled with a peace of mind. It bothered him that he couldn't feel this way when he was with LaToria.

After making two stops to pick up LaToria's food, he headed home with the system reverberating in the trunk. Tupac's "So Many Tears" came alive inside Trevon.

This ain't the life for me, I wanna change
But ain't no future right for me, I'm stuck in the
game.

He kept the song on repeat until he pulled up in his driveway. To his surprise, LaToria's Aston Martin was gone. Slowing to a stop beside her black Escalade, he was suddenly caught off guard when his smartphone rung. He took notice of the unknown number on the screen.

"Hello?" he answered.

"Hey handsome!"

Trevon leaned up in the seat. The voice sounded familiar, but he wasn't too sure. "Who is this?"

She laughed. "Turn around and you'll see."

Trevon twisted in the seat and was moved beyond words from the sight that greeted him.

THIS IS THE ORDER THAT WAHIDA'S BOOKS
SHOULD BE READ:

THUGS AND THE WOMEN WHO LOVE THEM
EVERY THUG NEEDS A LADY
THUG MATRIMONY
THUG LOVIN'
THE GOLDEN HUSTLA
JUSTIFY MY THUG
WHAT'S REALLY HOOD
PAYBACK IS A MUTHA
PAYBACK WITH YA LIFE
PAYBACK AIN'T ENOUGH
SLEEPING WITH THE ENEMY

CHECK OUT TITLES BY
WAHIDA CLARK PRESENTS PUBLISHING
TRUST NO MAN 1, 2 & 3 BY CASH
THIRSTY 1 & 2 BY MIKE SANDERS
THE GAME OF DECEPTION
BY VICTOR L. MARTIN
NUDE AWAKENING BY VICTOR L. MARTIN
KARMA WITH A VENGEANCE
BY TASH HAWTHORNE

KARMA: FOR THE LOVE OF MONEY
BY TASH HAWTHORNE
THE PUSSY TRAP 1 & 2 BY NE NE CAPRI
LICKIN' LICENSE 1 & 2 BY INTELLIGENT ALLAH
THE ULTIMATE SACRIFICE BY ANTHONY FIELDS
THE ULTIMATE SACRIFICE: LOVE IS PAIN
BY ANTHONY FIELDS
FEENIN' BY SERENITI HALL
STILL FEENIN' BY SERENITI HALL
A LIFE FOR A LIFE 1 & 2 BY MIKE JEFFRIES

TITLES FOR YOUNG ADULTS
THE BOY IS MINE! BY CHARMAINE WHITE
PLAYER HATER BY CHARMAINE WHITE
UNDER PRESSURE BY RASHAWN HUGHES
NINETY-NINE PROBLEMS
BY GLORIA-DOTSON LEWIS
SADE'S SECRET BY SPARKLE

WWW.WCLARKPUBLISHING.COM

NEVER READ A THUGS BOOK BEFORE?

GET A EXCLUSIVE!!!!

Sneak Peak of Chapter 1.
(Warning: You will be hooked.)
See what you've been missing!

-TEXT 58885 -

TYPE IN "THUGS,"
YOUR NAME AND EMAIL ADDRESS
AND GET THUGGED!!!!!

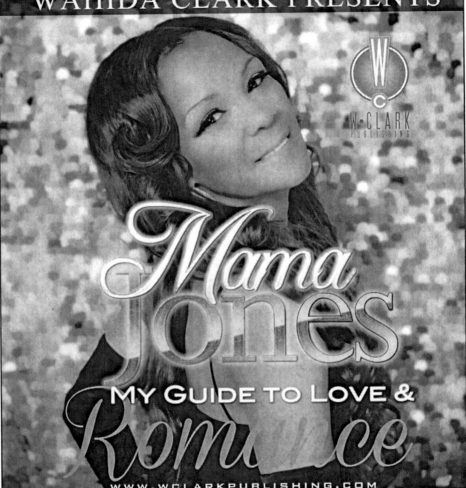

WAHIDA CLARK PRESENTS

SWAG

A NOVEL BY

ANGEL SANTOS

WAHIDA CLARK PRESENTS
The Devil's
GAME
A NOVEL
SHAWN 'JIHAD' TRUMP

FLIPPIN'

Hustle

A Novel by
TRAE MACKLIN

New York Times Bestselling Author of *Justify My Thug*

HONOR Thy THUG

WAHIDA CLARK